She clicked the mail  as it choked out the early image, and she tapped he mouse as the picture eme

It was someone with his back to her, hunched forward. His surroundings were vague, too much light. Gaia reached for the speaker, in case there was audio. There was. Staticky at first. Distant, fuzzy, then clearing.

Clearing . . .

"Maybe it's Heather, playing a joke," offered Ed. "To get even."

"I don't think so," said Gaia, her voice tight.

And then she heard his voice. . . .

"Gaia . . . ?"

Her heart seemed to freeze solid in her chest. No, no, no, no.

But the voice through the speaker repeated itself. "Gaia."

No! "Sam?"

As if he'd heard her, he turned to the camera, and suddenly there was Sam's face on the computer screen. One of his eyes was black-and-blue, swollen shut, and he looked frighteningly pale. Weak.

Ed angled his chair close to the desk. "Oh, shit."

Don't miss any books in this thrilling new series
from Pocket Books:

FEARLESS™

All Pocket Book titles are available by post from:
**Simon & Schuster Cash Sales, P.O. Box 29,
Douglas, Isle of Man IM99 1BQ**
Credit cards accepted. Please telephone 01624 675137,
Fax 01624 670923, Internet http://www.bookpost.co.uk
or email: bookshop@enterprise.net for details

FEARLESS™

FRANCINE PASCAL

RUN

An Imprint of Simon & Schuster UK Ltd
A Viacom Company
Africa House, 64-78 Kingsway, London WC2B 6AH

Produced by 17th Street Productions,
an Alloy Online, Inc. company
33 West 17th Street, New York, NY 10011

A CIP catalogue record for this book is
available from the British Library

ISBN 0671 03748 X

5 7 9 10 8 6 4

Printed by Cox & Wyman Ltd, Reading, Berkshire

RUN

Do you know what hell is?

I do.

It's not fire and brimstone. Not for me, anyway.

It's watching your hopes die.

It's watching the guy you love—the guy who makes you understand why that poor sucker built the Taj Mahal, why Juliet buried a dagger in her chest, why that Trojan king destroyed his entire fleet—making love to another girl. A girl you despise.

It's seeing your father—a man you believed was a superhero—for the first time after five long years only to discover he was a dishonorable creep show all along.

Hell is experiencing both of those things in one night. Hell is the way the ceiling looks above your bed when you open your eyes the next morning. Hell is the morning after that, when the ceiling looks just as hopeless, and you realize the pain

hasn't begun to fade and that
maybe it never will.

That is hell.

What is heaven?

I don't know.

I had an idea about it a couple of days ago, but that was before hope died.

If you happen to find out,
will you let me know?

One of his
eyes was
black-and-
blue,
swollen
shut, and he
looked
frighteningly
pale. Weak.

save

sam

"HELLO? ANYBODY UP THERE?"

Gaia had just stepped out of the shower when she heard the voice floating up the stairs to greet her. She wrapped a too-small towel around herself, went to the landing, and leaned into the stairwell. It was a familiar voice, but not one she expected to hear before eight o'clock in the morning.

You've Got Mail

"Ed?"

"Yeah."

"Um . . . what the hell are you doing here?"

She heard him laugh under his breath. "Just fine, thanks, and you?"

At the sound of his voice, a minute ray of happiness filtered down into the blackness of her mood. She hadn't spoken a word out loud since Saturday night, since everything . . . happened. Now it was Monday morning, and her words were so far back in her brain she had to hunt around for them. "N-Not that fine," she responded hoarsely. "I had . . ." How could she begin to convey the true horror that was her life? "Sort of a rough weekend."

"What else is new?"

She heard both affection and wariness in Ed's voice. He knew a "rough weekend" for Gaia meant more than teenage angst—that it would involve things like firearms and kickboxing.

4

"Tell me about it over breakfast," he called. "I brought bagels."

Her stomach grumbled loudly. One thing this city had going for it—authentic, fresh-out-of-the-oven bagels. They almost made up for the high price of Apple Jacks. She glanced down at herself and the small puddle forming under her feet. "I'm wearing a hand towel and a few cups of water," Gaia said, wishing Ella hadn't left early this morning, so that she could be disturbed by this exchange. At least Ella had taken George with her wherever she'd gone. Gaia disliked offending George as much as she enjoyed offending Ella.

"I repeat," said Ed, laughing again. **"C'mon down!"**

Gaia rolled her eyes, trying to ignore the undertones of the remark. Two minutes later, she'd slipped into her most-worn cargo pants and a gray T-shirt and was on her way downstairs, her hair dripping water over her shoulders. On the landing, she paused to study the familiar snapshot that hung in a frame there on the wall—the photograph George had taken so long ago of Gaia and her parents. Gaia had tried to get rid of it, but Ella insisted it remain. She squinted at it, looking hard at her father.

Her father. She'd seen him two nights ago. Actually seen him and spoken to him. *And decked him,* she reminded herself bitterly.

After that he'd disappeared—again.

Her stomach churned, both with confusion and

with sadness. Why had he shown up here after all this time? What could it mean?

Was it some paternal sixth sense that had dragged him back into her life? Did he somehow know she'd been on the verge of ditching her virginity, and he'd crawled out from whatever rock he'd been hiding under all these years to give her an old-fashioned heart-to-heart talk on morality, safe sex, and self-control?

Or was it just one more whacked-out coincidence in her life?

She leaned closer to the photo and stared into his eyes.

They appeared to be soft, kind, intelligent eyes—and the smile looked genuine. The man she'd met on Saturday night had not seemed genuine at all. The warmth and gentleness she saw in the picture had been missing from that man. He was different, somehow. Lesser.

Apparently abandoning your kid and living on the run could take a lot out of a person. In the kitchen, Gaia was met by the aroma of fresh bagels and hot coffee. Ed, who had positioned his chair close to the table, looked up from spreading cream cheese on a poppy seed bagel. "You didn't have to get dressed on my account."

She was annoyed at the blush his grin brought to her face. "Shut up." Her eyes narrowed. "How did you get in here, anyway?"

"Door was unlocked," Ed said. "You should really talk to your roomies about that. I mean this is a nice neighborhood, but why court robbery, or worse?"

Gaia collapsed into a chair. That was weird. George never left the door unlocked. Must've been another brilliant Ella maneuver.

"Do you think it's kismet that this place is handicap accessible?" Ed asked suddenly.

Gaia raised an eyebrow. "It's either kismet . . . or the building code."

"I'm serious," said Ed. "Do you have any idea how many places in this city aren't?"

She felt a pang of pity but squashed it fast. "So what's kismet got to do with it?"

"You happen to live in wheelchair-friendly digs. I happen to be in a wheelchair." Ed shrugged. "It's like the universe is arranging it so that we can hang out."

"The universe clearly has too much time on its hands." She sat down and pulled her knees up, leaning them against the edge of the table.

"Like lox?"

"Hate them."

"Then I'm glad I didn't buy any." Ed pushed a steaming cup of coffee across the table toward her. "Three sugars, no cream, right?"

Gaia nodded, refusing to be charmed by the fact that he remembered, and took a careful sip. She could feel him staring at her.

"You look like hell," he said, shaking a lock of brown hair back off his forehead. Suddenly he appeared to realize this was not a smart thing to say to a girl—any girl. "I mean . . . in a good way," he added lamely.

Gaia gave him a sidelong glance. "That's funny. I feel like hell." She took another, bolder sip of the hot coffee, letting the steamy liquid warm her from the inside.

"Now we're getting to it," Ed said, clasping his hands together and then cracking his knuckles. "You were unsurprisingly unfindable yesterday, Gaia. So let's hear it." He broke off a piece of bagel and pointed it at her. "Who was the lucky guy and how did the ceremonial shedding of the chastity belt go?"

Gaia ignored the bile rising in her throat, picked up a marble bagel, and took a gigantic bite. There was a reason she'd avoided Ed all day yesterday—the need to avoid forced emotional spillage. "Subtlety isn't exactly a talent of yours, is it, Ed?" she said with her mouth full.

"Look who's talking."

He had a point there. She studied Ed for a moment—the just-this-side-of-scruffy hair, the eager yet wary brown eyes, the dot of dried blood on his chin where he'd cut himself shaving. Gaia hated that she had to talk about this, but she did. She'd sucked Ed into the whole sorry situation when she confessed her virginity. Like it or not, over the past few weeks she had made Ed a friend, or something very close. He might as well know the truth.

Gaia closed her eyes. Shook her head. Sighed.

"It didn't happen," she said. And her whole body felt empty.

Ed dropped the knife onto the floor with a clatter. "It didn't?"

"Ed!" She opened her eyes and glared at him. "Think you can sound just a little more amused by that?"

"Sorry it didn't work out for you." Ed cleared his throat, and she could swear he was hiding a grin behind his steaming coffee. Some friend. "So what happened?" he asked.

Gaia took another aggressive bite of bagel. She chewed and swallowed before answering. "Let's just say I was witness to somebody beating me to it."

"Shut up!" Ed's eyes opened wide. "Gaia, tell me who we're talking about here. You can't keep me in this kind of suspense."

Say it, she commanded herself. Just say it. "It was Sam Moon."

A sudden shower of chewed bagel bits pelted Gaia's arms. "God, Ed! Food is to go in the mouth. *In*," Gaia said, brushing off her arms irritably.

"Do you mean you walked in on Sam and . . .

Heather?" Ed choked out while simultaneously attempting to wipe his mouth.

Somehow, saying it out loud gave Gaia a bit of distance. The words were vibrating in the fragrant air of the kitchen. Outside of her instead of inside. "Ironic, isn't it?" Gaia asked, flicking one last bagel wad off her elbow.

Ed looked as if he were watching his life flash before his eyes—backward and in 3-D with surround sound. Gaia had never seen his skin so pale. She'd forgotten for the moment that Heather meant something to Ed as well. A big something.

"Man." Ed let out a long rush of breath. His eyes were unfocused. "That had to suck."

It didn't suck. Sucking was getting busted for going seventy in a thirty-five-mile-an-hour zone. Sucking was losing a dollar in a Coke machine. Sucking didn't *hurt*.

"Could've been worse," she mumbled with a shrug. She wouldn't have believed it, except that it had actually gotten worse. The night had been full of mind-bending surprises. But she didn't need to share them now, if ever. They were highly dysfunctional family matters to be discussing over breakfast.

"What could be worse than walking in on the object of your seduction in bed with your mortal enemy?"

It was a decent question. Gaia was saved from needing to explain by the sound of the phone ringing.

Ed reached behind him, snatched the cordless from

the counter, then slid it across the table to Gaia. She hit the button and held the receiver to her ear. "Hello?"

At first, nothing.

"Hello?"

"Gaia Moore?"

Her eyes narrowed. "Yeah? Who is this?"

The voice was distorted, like something from a horror movie. "Check your e-mail." It was a command. Maybe even a threat.

She felt as if ice were forming in her veins. "Who is this?"

"Check your e-mail," the voice growled.

The line went dead.

Gaia was on her feet, running for George's computer, which, luckily, he always left on. When she reached the den, she flung herself into the chair and punched at the keyboard. Ed, maneuvering his chair through the rooms, appeared soon after.

"What's going on?"

Gaia was too morbidly curious to answer. She clicked the mail icon and stared at the screen as it choked out the early, cryptic shadows of a video image, and she tapped her fingers impatiently on the mouse as the picture emerged . . . slowly . . . slowly . . .

It was someone with his back to her, hunched forward. His surroundings were vague, too much light. Gaia reached for the speaker, in case there was audio. There was. Staticky at first. Distant, fuzzy, then clearing.

Clearing . . .

"Maybe it's Heather, playing a joke," offered Ed. "To get even."

Gaia was so intent on the image she barely heard him. "I don't think so."

Over the computer speakers she heard his voice. . . .

"Gaia . . . ?"

Her heart seemed to freeze solid in her chest. No, no, no, no.

But the voice through the speaker repeated itself. "Gaia."

No! "Sam?"

As if he'd heard her, he turned to the camera, and suddenly there was Sam's face on the computer screen. One of his eyes was black-and-blue, swollen shut, and he looked frighteningly pale. Weak.

Ed angled his chair close to the desk. "Oh, shit."

Sam's face vanished, replaced by a blank screen, and then there was a blast of static from the speakers as the same distorted voice addressed her. "Gaia Moore. You can see from this footage that we have a mutual friend. Sadly, he's not feeling well at the moment. Did you know Sam is a diabetic? No, I would imagine you didn't. . . ."

Ed stared at the blank screen. "Who the hell is it?"

Gaia shushed him with a sharp hiss as a graphic began to appear on the screen—a message snaking its way from the right side, one letter at a time:

C . . . A . . . N . . . Y . . . O . . . U . . .

The voice continued as the letters slid into view. "He's well enough for the moment, but around, oh, say, ten o'clock this evening he'll be needing his insulin, quite desperately. And that, my darling Gaia, is where you come in. You must pass a series of tests. You must pass these tests by ten o'clock tonight. If you do not, we will not wait for the diabetes to take over. If you do not pass these tests in the allotted time . . ."

The graphic slithered by: S . . . A . . . V . . . E . . .

". . . we will kill him."

S . . . A . . . M . . . ?

For a moment the question trembled there on the dark screen. CAN YOU SAVE SAM? Then the letters went spinning off into the infinite background, and another message appeared in an eye-searing flash of brightness. It read:

You will find on your front step a videotape.
You will play it during your first-period class.
DO NOT view the tape prior to showing it in school.

Without warning, the e-mail broadcast returned, showing a close-up of Sam's beaten face, his frightened eyes, his mouth forming a word, and the word came screaming through the speaker in Sam's voice.

"Gaia!"

Then nothing. The image and the audio were gone,

and the computer whirred softly until George's sickening screen saver—a scanned-in photo of Ella—returned to the screen.

Gaia sprang up from the chair and flew to the front door, which she flung open. The early October air sparkled, and the neighborhood was just coming alive with people on their way to work and school. Gaia paid no attention. Her eyes searched the front stoop until they found the package.

She lunged for it.

Gaia had no idea who had done this. She had no idea why. But she wasn't about to ask questions.

In that instant, it didn't matter that Sam had had sex with Heather or that he didn't return Gaia's overwhelming love for him and probably never would.

Sam life was in danger. For now, that was all that mattered.

"WHAT ARE YOU DOING?" ED demanded, wheeling himself out from the exit under the stoop, afraid for a moment that the package might explode in her hands.

The Knight

But Gaia had grabbed her ever-present messenger bag and was down

14

the steps. Ed aimed his chair to the left, toward the sidewalk. He could barely see Gaia over the row of potted shrubs as she sprinted away.

He caught up to her three corners later. One good thing about being in a wheelchair—even New York drivers slowed to let you cross the street.

She was bouncing on the balls of her feet, waiting for the light to change.

"Gaia, hold on. You can't just go to school and put that thing in the VCR!"

She didn't turn to face him. "Watch me."

"What if it . . . I don't know . . . what if it starts spewing out poisonous gas or something?" Ed offered.

"This isn't a *Batman* episode, Ed!" Gaia spat out, glancing over her shoulder. "What do you think, the Penguin sent that e-mail?"

"No, but somebody just as wacko did!"

"**Somebody who's got Sam.**" Her voice was grim. Determined.

"Yeah, I get that. But we need to think about this. You don't know what's on that tape." He shook his head. "Okay, I admit, toxic vapor is a little extreme. But this whole thing is freaky, and I'm just saying we should be careful."

"You be careful," she snapped. "I'll be quick."

"Do you *never* think before you act?"

"Ed! Listen!" She grabbed the armrests of his

wheelchair and leaned over to look him directly in the eyes. She was so close he could see the pores in the perfect skin around her nose. Her hair was still wet against her cheeks. "I don't know who is doing this or why," she said. "But I have to help Sam."

In the next second he watched, helpless, as she flung herself out into the middle of traffic. A cab swerved. A UPS truck hit the brakes. A bike messenger careened off a mailbox.

But she made it.

He expected her to go right on running, but when she hit the opposite sidewalk, she turned and looked at him.

It was probably the fastest look in the history of eye contact, but that look was loaded. It was part defiance, part desperation, and part apology.

"Go!" he shouted, his voice raw. "I'll see you there."

She nodded almost imperceptibly, then took off down the street.

He followed as fast as his confinement allowed. Thinking.

She wanted to sleep with Sam. Sam Moon. But she hadn't. It had taken complete self-control to keep from popping a wheelie in his chair when she'd confessed that. Saturday night had been torture—the thought of her in someone else's arms, of someone else kissing her, had kept him awake all night. Awake and angry and sick to his stomach.

Because he loved her desperately. In mind, in spirit, in body. He wanted her.

So what if she wanted Sam? Seeing him with Heather must have cured that, right? The fact that she was rushing off to his rescue, no questions asked, just meant she was noble. One more thing to love about her.

Ed's remark about the universe setting them up came back to him, and he cringed. Stupid. Childish. Pathetic.

Yet on some level he'd meant it. He'd found her, that first day in the hall at school. She'd been so lost, and so not wanting to be lost. Ed knew how lost felt. He'd felt it every day since he'd first sat in this chair. Every day he was set apart.

He approached school and entered the crush of people. He imagined Gaia in her first-period classroom, slamming the mysterious video into the VCR. What the hell is on the tape? he wondered, feeling panic press into him.

And if he had to, could he rescue her from it?

He smiled bitterly at the ridiculous image. Sir Edward of Useless Limbs, the knight in not-so-shining armor, rushing in to rescue the fair Gaia, Lady of Brutal Ass Kickings.

Remember that, pal? Three punks in one shot. And

without even having to touch up her lip gloss afterward. His lady had no need for a knight. And, anyway, knights rode horses, not chairs.

He broke from the pack of students and rolled toward the handicapped entrance.

As he did on every other day of the school year, Ed entered the building alone.

To: ELJ
From: L
Date: October 11
File: 776244
Subject: Gaia Moore

She is even more beautiful up close. And far more dangerous. For now, we proceed as planned. The trials have begun. We will test her limits. I want to see how far she will go for this boy. What she will risk. How much she is willing to lose.

The boy suffers, but it is all in the name of authenticity.

I have no doubt she will succeed on her own; however, if any complications should arise to impede her various quests, I will arrange for assistance. Her safety, as ever, is of utmost importance. She must not fail—for all roads lead to me. Tonight I will secure my position in her life. There is much to alter. Much to gain.

To: L
From: ELJ
Date: October 11
File: 776244
Subject: Gaia Moore

I understand what is expected of me. The note is already written and waiting to be planted. Other objects with regard to this aspect of the plan are also in place.

GN and I will leave the city early. He will not be there to help her or to interfere in any way. He will not suspect a thing.

Tonight I will meet the pawn and see that he is where we need him to be, and when.

Sam's face. Sam's bruised face. It came out of that computer at me like a kick to the teeth. And then he had to go and call my name like that.

I wonder if fear feels anything like desperation. Because that's what I felt when his voice came reverberating out of those speakers.

He called *my* name.

This probably sounds totally inappropriate, but there was a moment there . . . There was a moment there when I was glad he was calling *me*. And I can think of only two possible reasons why.

Reason #1. The kidnapper told Sam he was zapping his image to *my* computer, so who else's name *would* he say?

But I doubt the kidnapper is giving him any information pertaining to his rescue, so the chances of his knowing he was even being filmed are pretty

slim. Besides, he doesn't know
about my . . . talents, or my
weird life, so why would he be
calling out to me for help? It's
not like he'd expect me to be
able to come crashing in and
kick his captor's ass—which I
would do in a heartbeat, if only
I knew where he was. So that
brings me to:

Reason #2. He's thinking of
me. (Could it be?)
   Thinking of me insofar as a
guy in hypoglycemic shock (or
whatever it's called when dia-
betics need insulin) who may
also be suffering a concussion
can think.
   Like maybe he screamed "Gaia"
because Gaia was the first thing
that came to his mind.
   Gaia. *Me.* Gaia.
   I don't know.
   What I do know, though, is
this: As long as there's an
ounce of strength in my body, I
am going to do everything I

possibly can to do what that son-of-a-bitch kidnapper chal-lenged me to do.

I'm going to save Sam.

And when I find out who did this to him, I'm going to take the guy down.

She told
herself the
only thing
independent
that
film
mattered was
that she'd
passed the
first test.

"NO, MAN! NO, MAN, *PLEASE!* DON'T!"

CJ closed his eyes as Tarick lifted one rock-solid fist and slammed it against CJ's skull. His eye felt as if it had been dislodged from its socket, and his mouth instantly filled with blood.

Weird Shit

"You let her go?" Tarick shouted, coming at CJ again. This time he wrenched CJ's arm—the one in the sling. The one with the bullet hole in it. The pain shot through his entire body like an explosion, and everything went blurry. CJ sank to the grimy concrete floor on his knees and then fell forward, savoring the feel of the cold, grainy surface against his cheek. It smelled like burnt cigarettes and blood. CJ knew it was the last smell he'd ever experience if he didn't do something.

"Kill him." Tarick's voice.

"Now."

"No! No! Wait!"

He heard them loading the gun.

"I can still do it!" CJ shouted through the pain.

Suddenly he was being wrenched to his feet, and Tarick used one beefy hand to push CJ up against the wall by his neck. "We should have let you bleed to death in the first place, you useless piece of shit." Tarick spat in CJ's face, but CJ couldn't move a muscle. He just let the gob slide down the side of his nose and onto his chin.

"I can still do it," he repeated pathetically, choking on the words. Joey was hovering behind Tarick, gun clenched in his hand. He didn't even look sad or scared. He just looked ready.

Tarick released him and he fell to the ground, sputtering for breath. He bent over at the waist, thought better of taking his eyes off Joey, and forced himself to straighten up.

"Please, Tarick," CJ said, his eyes stinging. "Weird shit is always happening around this bitch. Guys with guns, like she's got a protector or something."

Tarick laughed, showing his yellowed teeth and flashing the stud that pierced his tongue. "This isn't a storybook, CJ," Tarick said. "She don't have a fairy godmother."

Joey cocked the gun.

"Please, man," CJ said, trying hard not to whimper. "Just give me one more chance. I won't let you down again."

Tarick's eyes roamed over CJ's broken and battered body. He sucked at his teeth, ran a hand over his shaved and tattooed head. He glanced at Joey, then looked back at CJ.

"All right, man," Tarick said with a quick nod. "You get one more chance."

CJ let out a sigh of relief and closed his eyes. Then Tarick's voice cut through the darkness, his breath impossibly close to CJ's ear.

"Screw it up again, and I kill you myself."

HEATHER GANNIS DID NOT WALK SO

Floating

much as float. With her delicate chin tipped upward slightly, she moved purposefully but gracefully through the posthomeroom throng. The look of disdain on her pretty face was to remind the Gap-clad masses that she was, and would always be, their superior. Even if she didn't necessarily feel like it. They were the ones who'd elevated her to that status. She was the one who had to struggle daily to perpetuate the illusion.

She floated, seemingly high on her own significance, weightless in the knowledge that she, and she alone, had the best hair, the best blouse, the best ass.

She was Heather Gannis, too ethereal to simply walk.

That was how they saw her, anyway, and that was what they expected, maybe even needed. And she was the one they'd elected to provide it for them.

Sometimes she thought she'd be willing to chuck the whole popularity thing in a heartbeat. Other times, having swarms of admirers had its perks.

And so she'd float.

Today, though, she had to work harder than usual to pull it off. Today she was dealing with stuff. Big-time confusion. Insecurity—not about her beauty or her position at school, of course. Insecurity beyond the ordinary is-there-lipstick-on-my-teeth variety.

And Heather's self-doubt came in the form of the same pitiful little mutant who'd put her in the hospital. Gaia Moore.

What kind of name was that, anyway? Guy-uh. Sounded like a Cro-Magnon grunt rather than a name.

And Cro-Magnon girl had ruined everything. Shocker.

Saturday night had started out perfect. Then it had gotten even better.

She'd been in Sam's arms—securing what was hers, giving him what he wanted before Gaia had the chance to make an offer of her own.

Heather's motives for Saturday night had been part romance, part strategy. Sleeping with Sam would cement their relationship—take it to the next level. She was reasonably certain that Sam would forget Gaia completely if he believed Heather was committed enough to make him her first.

Sam wouldn't really be her first, of course—she'd lost her virginity to Ed long ago—but he'd *believe* that he was. She'd (briefly) considered telling him the truth, but decided "first" sounded so much more devoted than "next." Ed was her secret, and she was going to keep it that way.

But Gaia had her grubby little hooks in Ed, too. It made Heather's skin crawl to think about that. Ed followed Gaia around like a damn puppy dog.

She realized she was aching to see Gaia, maybe right now, in the hallway, where she could create some big, ugly scene that would make her look great and Gaia look even more pathetic than before.

She remembered with the small section of her brain in which she stored information about school that Gaia was in her first-period class. Fine. She could destroy her there just as easily. Smaller audience, but better acoustics.

Heather's mind spun (but she kept floating) and images of Sam, catapulting off the bed to chase after Gaia, burned in her mind. The Slim-Fast bar she'd eaten for breakfast threatened to come up. What had he been thinking? What was wrong with him, leaving her for Gaia, and just on the brink of . . . well, of everything?

But that bitch—that disgusting, creepy little bitch had shown up, and Sam had freaked.

On the upside, Gaia had looked absolutely miserable upon catching them in the act. Maybe now she'd get the message and back off. The girl had proof now, proof that Sam and Heather were the real deal. Of course, Sam's running after her might have given Gaia cause to wonder. . . .

Damn him! Why had he left? And why hadn't he called? That had been Saturday. This was Monday! No call, no personal appearance. She could have been home crying all weekend and he didn't even care.

A chill shot through her. What the hell had taken place when Sam caught up to Gaia Saturday? Had she said something, done something, to override Heather's sexual surrender?

Was there anything that *could* override sex for a guy? She doubted it, but still. Evidently Gaia had some weird power over Sam. Had she been able to use that power on Saturday, even as his hair was still tousled from Heather's own fingers?

Heather mentally checked her expression. No creases. No frowning. She had to look distant, aloof, as calm as always or else they might suspect. She lowered her eyelids slightly, pushed out her lower lip—sexy, sullen, unconcerned, and floating. Christ, this was getting old.

They called out to her, waved. Occasionally she'd reply, but not often enough to give them any substantial hope. And tomorrow she'd do it again.

And tomorrow. And tomorrow.

Shit! That reminded her. She had a Shakespeare quiz later this morning, and she hadn't even opened her notebook. What was it old Willie had said about the moon? The inconstant moon. Sam Moon. Inconstant, big time. Changeable. Fickle. And in love with Gaia Moore?

Maybe.

Heather entered her first-period class and immediately scanned the room to see if Gaia was there. To her amazement, the loser was actually present, actually had the nerve to show her face! Heather prepared herself to deploy her patented secret weapon—a look of death that could make even the thumb-heads on the wrestling team shiver in their sneakers—but Gaia seemed to be looking right through her.

Oh, this one was good. Most girls who found themselves on Heather's shit list would be groveling already. But this freak of nature had the audacity to diss her. On some level Heather was actually impressed. It was almost a relief to know there was someone who didn't shed all self-respect the minute Heather threw her a look.

Okay, so it was impressive. But it still pissed her off.

Heather slammed her books onto her desk, accepted some hellos from neighboring students, then noticed that the classroom television was on. The screen was blank—the same bright blue Tommy Hilfiger used last spring—and the VCR light was blinking.

Thank God! Heather thought. A video was about all she could handle this morning. Probably something about the Civil War. Wait. This was economics, not history. Okay, something boring about supply and demand, then. Perfect.

She wouldn't even have to watch. She could study for Shakespeare and write vicious things about Gaia on the desktop. And wonder if Sam was out of her life for good now.

And if he was, was he in Gaia's life instead? Losing him would be bad. Losing him to her would be unbearable.

God, did that little witch actually believe she could do battle with her? Did she think she was better than Heather Gannis? And if she thought she was, how long would it be before the rest of the people in this school—flock of sheep that they were—began thinking it, too?

She didn't want to think about this. Not now. She wanted to get her mind off Gaia and Sam. She'd allow herself one nasty piece of desktop graffiti, then maybe she'd watch the stupid video after all.

SITTING THROUGH HOMEROOM WAS

torture. What could the cassette possibly contain? Wicked neo-Nazi propaganda? Gang recruitment information? Or maybe something closer to home—a biographical account of her messed-up life, edited for the sole purpose of humiliating her in public? But since Gaia had no idea who'd kidnapped Sam, she couldn't even begin to pinpoint a motive, and therefore could not even venture a guess as to what purpose this video, this **"test,"** might serve.

She was about to find out. First period. The moment of truth.

If anyone was surprised that the video was starting before the teacher was present, they didn't mention it. Someone at the back of the room hit the lights. Gaia glanced over her shoulder and saw it was Ed, who'd just arrived. He was supposed to be in English now, wasn't he? But here he was, for moral support.

First bagels, now this. She felt a small cyclone of warmth in her stomach. So this was what friends did for you, huh? Gaia squelched the warmth. She couldn't risk getting used to it.

Ed shot her a look that was part encouragement, part panic. She turned away fast.

The blue screen gave way to a sudden blast of snowy static, then the scene focused.

It appeared to be a wide-angle shot of the upper half of a bedroom. The room was dimly lit, but Gaia could make out posters on the walls, an NYU pennant, a wide window with the blinds pulled.

And there were noises.

The usual New York background noises, of course—distant sirens, car horns, blaring radios. But over those came the more interesting noises.

Sounds like soft growling and deep sighs, sounds that seemed to caress each other.

Now where had she heard that before?

And then the camera panned down, pulling a form into focus.

It was an odd angle from which to film. Even Gaia, with her lack of experience in both filmmaking and lovemaking, knew that. The subjects were unidentifiable. There was a broad back, encircled from below by svelte, ribbonlike arms that tapered into delicate hands and graceful fingers. But the camera angle was designed to provide no clear view of either face.

The noises deepened, grew urgent, began to resemble words.

"Oh. Oh my—"

All the air seemed to flee Gaia's lungs at once. She knew that voice. And now that she looked closer, the blanket covering the bottom half of the couple looked pretty familiar as well.

They, them, him, her.

Gaia gripped the edges of her desk. Shit! What should she do? Let it run? Or jump up (assuming she could actually get her body to jump, since she seemed to be paralyzed) and turn the thing off? After all, sooner or later she'd be making her own cameo in this film.

The class was catching on now, and the howling began. As far as Gaia could tell, they hadn't recognized the female lead just yet. The star herself, in response to the provocative remarks of her classmates, had only just looked up from something she was scribbling on her desktop.

The graceful fingers were now clawing at the broad back.

Out of the corner of her eye, Gaia could see Heather studying the screen. Heather's first instinct, it appeared, was to smile. Hell, it was funny! Funny, as long as it wasn't your inaugural sexual liaison being screened in first-period advanced-placement economics.

Gaia kept her eyes slanted in Heather's direction and watched as the perfect smile flickered once, then vanished. Realization flared in Heather's eyes just as her video incarnation was uttering her first line of dialogue.

"Oh my God . . . Sam!"

To which oh-my-God-Sam replied, *"Heather!"*

Busted!

Gaia snapped her attention back to the screen. Sundance, eat your heart out. Whoever this independent-film director was, he certainly had a flair for timing, because it was at this point that AP econ was allowed to enjoy the first close-up shot of the movie.

And it featured none other than Heather Gannis, perspiring elegantly, eyelids fluttering, flawless teeth clamped down on her lower lip.

The class exploded in reaction. Some of them shrieked in disbelief. Some laughed, some applauded wildly. Most just gasped. Heather, in a surprising gesture that made Gaia feel almost sorry for her, covered her face with one trembling hand and began to sob.

Gaia wondered absently if anyone had seen her stick the tape in the VCR. If they had, this could get really ugly really fast. As if it weren't ugly enough already.

Two of Heather's girlfriends sprang to her side, ostensibly trying to comfort her.

"Somebody eject it!" one of them demanded.

"No pun intended!" replied someone on a choke of laughter.

Another of Heather's sidekicks—a girl named Megan—got up and moved toward the front of the room to turn off the television. Was it just Gaia's imagination, or did Megan seem to be taking her sweet time getting there?

AP econ was treated to a few additional renditions of "Oh my God, Sam!" before the electric-green-painted acrylic nail of Megan's index finger connected with the off button.

Instantly the class shut up, as if some cosmic off button had been punched as well.

The room went completely silent. Silent, except for the muffled gulping of Heather's crying.

Shame washed over Gaia.

Worse than fear, she guessed. It had to be.

Suddenly Gaia found herself silently pleading with Heather to go: Run. Get out. The silence pulsed as she kept her eyes glued to her desktop, willing her sworn enemy to escape. The girl was a bitch, sure, and a monster. But nobody, not even Heather, deserved this.

And then, as if she had sensed Gaia's unspoken plea, Heather catapulted out of her seat and stumbled toward the door. Megan and the other two handmaidens went running after Heather, looking appropriately concerned. But just before Megan disappeared through the door, she turned and fixed Gaia with a glare that Megan probably thought was menacing.

She knew. Which meant that in about 1.5 seconds Heather would know, too.

Ed made his exit as well, and the teacher picked that moment to arrive, stepping through the door but looking over her shoulder into the corridor.

"What's happened to Miss Gannis?" she asked.

"I think she lost something," one of the boys answered, biting back laughter. A giggle rippled through the room.

The shame swelled. Who was the monster now?

"Turn to page thirty-four," the teacher said.

In the wake of the X-rated video they'd just seen, the teacher's lecture on inflation and upward trends incited a few scattered chuckles and snorts. But Gaia was barely aware of them.

Numbly she wondered what Ed would say. He might be furious with her. After all, he and Heather had a history. Or maybe he'd just say, "I told you so," which, of course, would be even worse.

She told herself the only thing that mattered to her was that she'd passed the first test, and that Sam was one step closer to safety.

She hoped.

GAIA HUNG BACK AFTER THE BELL,

High School Drama

until the classroom had emptied. Then she snatched the video and stuffed it into her beat-up messenger bag. She'd destroy it later. Crush it, or burn it, or something equally absolute. The last thing she needed was for it to wind up playing 24/7 on the Internet—the scene of her nightmares playing out for the global community's entertainment.

Ed was waiting for her in the hall.

So were Heather and a sea of salivating spectators.

Gaia took one look into Heather's very wet, very red, very livid eyes and considered walking right past her, rather than enduring the obligatory scene of high school drama that everyone was expecting. But Gaia stayed rooted in place. She'd done what she was about to be accused of. Some remote part of her was eager to clothe herself in blame. Maybe even needed to.

"Where did you get it?" Heather asked, her voice surprisingly even. "Where did you get that tape?"

"I found it," Gaia answered. True. There was the requisite murmur from the crowd at this stunning tidbit of noninformation.

Heather's perfectly lined eyes narrowed. "You're not even going to deny it was you?"

"No." Another murmur, this one louder.

"Are you going to explain?" Heather took a step closer. Megan and the other sidekicks exchanged a look that said things were about to get interesting.

"I didn't know what was on the tape," Gaia said with a shrug. Also true.

Heather let out a noise that was somewhere between a shriek and asphyxiation. "Tell me where you got it," she said. She was right in Gaia's face. The tangy sweetness of her perfume made Gaia's nose itch. The girl was brave. But then, she did have the entire school behind her. And she didn't know what Gaia was capable of. Not that Gaia had any intention of letting Heather find out—let alone the ever-growing crowd.

"I already told you," Gaia said.

And then Heather pushed her. It was the kind of push that normally wouldn't have affected Gaia in the slightest—had she been expecting it. But Heather had caught her off guard, and Gaia stumbled backward until her shoulders pressed into the wall.

The crowd let out a little "ooh." Gaia righted herself, standing up straight for the first time in recent memory.

Heather took the slightest step back, betrayed herself with the smallest flinch. Gaia was sure she was the only one who saw it.

"What kind of psychotic freak are you?" Heather said loudly, shoving Gaia again.

This time Gaia didn't budge. "The kind of psychotic freak you don't want to push again," she said under her breath.

There were a few things Heather could do at this point, and Gaia watched her face with interest as

Heather ran through the possibilities in a fraction of a second. Where would the roulette ball land?

Would Heather:

A) call Gaia's bluff and push her again?

B) lose her shit and run?

Or

C) back off with some catty remark, thereby making herself look like the bigger person and the victor?

"You're not worth it," Heather said.

So it was going to be C.

Good choice.

There was a disappointed muttering from the male contingent, a sigh of relief from the females. Heather backed up, fixing a wry smile on her face. "You do realize that your life at this school is beyond over," she said, then snorted a bitter laugh. "Not that it ever started."

The masses laughed and scoffed and made general noises of agreement.

Gaia said nothing. Moved not an inch.

Heather took this as cause to smile even wider, and turned to her friends. "Show's over."

And with that the crowd dispersed, punctuating Heather's threat with their own disgusted looks and comments.

Gaia didn't bother to look like she cared. She didn't care. Heather's idea of hell was social failure, but Gaia knew better. For Gaia, the ridicule of her fellow high school students was about as distressing as a hair in her spaghetti. Gaia took a deep breath. She'd let Heather have her moment. That was the best she could do in the way of an apology.

Now she could get back to what really mattered. Sam.

ED WAS THE ONLY ONE LEFT. ED

Close to Home

and the few hallway stragglers who'd unluckily been too late to catch the action.

"You were right," Gaia said sharply before he could open his mouth. "I shouldn't have shown it without a preview."

Ed shrugged. "You didn't know. You couldn't have known."

Gaia's shoulders slumped. "Heather ..."

"Good call not pummeling her, by the way," Ed said matter-of-factly.

"Yeah, well, she had enough for one morning."

Ed reached up, took Gaia's hand, and squeezed it. Gaia `pulled away instantly,` but Ed didn't even blink. "I wouldn't feel too bad about putting Heather in a compromising position if I were you," he said. "I think that was more Sam's responsibility, anyway, if you know what I mean."

"Ed!" Gaia said tersely.

"Sorry." He raised his hands in surrender.

Gaia adjusted her bag on her shoulder. "Forget Heather. Here's what I don't get—the e-mail said that showing the video was a test. So what did it prove? I mean, what could humiliating Heather have possibly gained for the kidnapper? If the video made some kind of demand or threat, that would make sense. But this was just . . . humiliating. And cruel."

Ed nodded. "I know what you mean. It was more like a practical joke. A demonic one."

"Maybe the kidnapper just wanted to see if I'd follow directions," Gaia said, glancing over her shoulder at the rapidly emptying hallway. "Which brings me to—"

"To how the kidnapper is going to know what you do and don't do," said Ed, finishing the thought for her.

Gaia sighed. "I guess we can safely figure that I am under `constant surveillance`."

"Guess so."

Gaia sighed. "Creepy."

"Very."

"So where's the next test?" Gaia said, glaring at the grate-covered hallway clock. "If I have to jump

44

through a bunch of hoops before ten o'clock tonight, why didn't they just give them all to me at once?" She was bouncing up and down again, raring to go. She didn't like this feeling of being watched, of being manipulated, of being out of control.

Sam was out there somewhere, suffering, and there was nothing she could do about it until these assholes decided to contact her. How was she supposed to handle this?

"I could be *done* by now," she said, watching the seconds tick by.

"You know what worries me?" Ed asked, his forehead creased. "Whoever this guy is, he seems to be striking very close to home."

"What do you mean?" Gaia wrapped her arms around herself. The anticipation was making her feel like she was going to explode through her skin.

"I mean you got lucky," Ed said, maneuvering his chair around a line of people waiting for the water fountain. "You went to Sam's room with a mission, remember? It could just as easily have been you on that tape, Gaia."

Gaia tightened her grip on herself. She hadn't thought of that.

"Who knows? Maybe it was *supposed* to be you." Ed lowered his voice as a group of teachers passed. "And that would mean that whoever planted the camera in Sam's room has a serious inside line on you. I mean, even beyond constant surveillance. It's almost like he can read your mind. This can't be just about Sam."

Gaia checked the clock again. "It's not like I know anything about Sam." *Except that I love him . . . and I hate him,* she added silently as the contents of the video burned in her mind.

"But if the kidnapper wanted money or attention or something, why would they contact you?" Ed asked. "Wouldn't they send a ransom note to his parents or something? This whole thing is pretty random."

Gaia stopped walking and stared at a crack in the cinder block wall just above Ed's head. "So you think it's about me." Not a question.

"You're the one with all the secrets, Gaia," Ed said, lifting his chin in an obvious attempt to arrest her line of vision. "Whatever they are."

Gaia scanned the hallway again. No one suspicious. Nothing out of place. "Aren't you glad I won't let you ask questions? You're safer not knowing."

"Somehow I don't feel all that safe." Ed started moving again, narrowly missing the open-toed sandal of an oblivious freshman.

"God! Where are they?" Gaia blurted, covering her watch with her hand as if she could make time stop. "What if they sent another e-mail?" She started bouncing again, as if she were a boxer psyching herself up for a fight. "I can't just stand around like this. I have to find him."

They continued down the hall in silence, Gaia staring every passerby in the eye, glancing over her shoulder every third of a second. When she reached her second-period class, which she had no intention of sitting still through, the teacher met her in the doorway.

"Ms. Moore, I just received a note asking me to send you to the main office to pick up a package," Mrs. Reingold said with a vapid smile.

Gaia's heart gave a leap of actual joy. *Good. Let's get on with it.*

"Receiving gifts at school, are we?" Mrs. Reingold continued. "Do we find this appropriate?"

Gaia was about to tell the teacher exactly what we could do with our idea of appropriate when Ed pinched her leg.

"You must have left your lunch at home this morning," Ed said.

"Yeah," Gaia snapped, glancing at the withered old teacher. "My parents don't like me to go through the day without three squares."

When Mrs. Reingold closed the classroom door, Gaia spun on her heel and practically flew to the main office. Ed was right behind her.

She burst into the office, told the principal's secretary who she was, and was handed a sealed envelope.

Ed was waiting for her back in the hall. For a moment she just stared at the envelope.

"Please tell me you're about to read the nominees for Best Picture," said Ed, his face a little pale.

"I wish." Gaia leaned against the water fountain. She slid her finger beneath the flap and tugged, then pulled out a sheet of paper and began to read it aloud: "'Kudos on the successful completion of Test One.'" She looked up from the paper and frowned at Ed. "Kudos? Oh, great. So the guy's not only a maniac, he's a dork."

"A dangerous dork, Gaia. Keep reading."

Wrrrzzzzzzzz.

I am Sam Moon.

They said my name. I heard them. Good, because maybe I forgot it. Sam Moon, Sam Moon, Sam Moon.

Sam Moon.

Wrrrzzzzzzzz. Clank. Wrrrzzzzzzzz.

They grabbed me. That much I know. But who? Why?

Wrrrzzzzzzzz. Clank.

If that damned noise would just . . . stop. It comes in through a window I can't see. That . . . noise. That . . . grinding, scraping, scratching, humming, rumbling.

WrrrzzzzzzClankWrrrzzzzzz.

NearFarAlwaysLouderSofter . . .

Wrrrzzzzzzzz. God! Numbing my brain.

Not just the noise the questions my own questions I have never wondered so hard it's making me queasy all this not knowing my blood is screaming it's pounding in my temples I can taste my own bile I keep

shaking and I want to peel my
skin off—

 And I want to kiss Gaia.

 Did I? Once? I did, I think.
She was soft. Her eyes took me.
Took me right in. Nothing bluer,
ever. Nothing so generous, or
alone and . . .

 Wrrrzzzzzzzz clank wrrzz.

 Shit, what the hell happened
to my face? Oh Yeah, Guy With A
Fist With A Ring. And the voice.
Not the Fist's voice, somebody
else's.

 Pokey? Smokey? Low Key? Loki.

 His voice, then the fist.
Damnthathurt.

 Then how come they haven't
killed me yet? Or have they?
Maybe I'm supposed to be heading-
forthelight already.

 Jesus, I'm losing it. I'm not
dead. Okay? *I'mnotdead.* Just . . .
focus. Right, that's right. Focus.

 I amSam MoonI am Sam . . . Sam
I am.

 Remember? Yes. I remember. I
am sitting on my mother's lap

yesterday last week now later.
Athousandyearsago. Letters are
new, words are strange. I am
small—

And safeAnd she is reading to
me. Something about . . . what?

Eggs? Yes. And Ham. Green Eggs
and Ham. Yes! And Sam I am.

I said,

Sam *I* am

and we laughed and laughed and
laughed.

God I want to laugh again.
Now. Right now.

*Wrrrzzzzzzzz clank
wrrrzzzzzzzz.* Laugh!

Do I remember how? Try. You
can't laugh if you're dead. Be
alive. Laugh.

Try. I must be laughing, because look how they're looking at
me.

Uhhg. Something burns my
throat then my tongue then my
lips. Laughing hurts.

And I'm vomiting. I'm puking.

That happens. Diabetic. Me.

It's warm on my chin slick

smearing down onto my shirt. It reeks. Bad.

Someone comes, cleans me up. Not gentle. Not like Mom did.

Mom?

Wrrrzzzzzzzzclankwrrrzzzzzzzz.

The noise, damn it! It's messing up the story. Inahousewitha mouseinaboxwithafox.

Wrrrzzzzzzzzz. Clank. Wrrzz.

Focus. Remember . . . how did it start? Where was I before I was here? What was I thinking before I couldn't think? Focus . . .

Heat. And shoulders. And a silky throat.

Heather. Me. Together. So together. Mmmmmm . . . almost good. But I'm wishing beyond it. I'm wishing for Gaia.

Wrrrzzzzzzzz clank wrrzz.

And then . . . Gaia.

Gaia. Jesus. Gaia. No, don't go . . . I'm sorry. And then . . . running. Darkness and streetlights and . . . where? Where did she go? And then the arm across my chest, the hands around my throat.

And *wrrrzzzzzzzz* I'm here again, over the noise again. Still.

Oh, God. What the hell is happening? I don't know. I can't know. Knowing is somewhere else. And it all fades into the noise.

Wrrrzzzzzzzz clank.

Gaia?

Wrrrzzzzzzzz . . .

. . . zzzzzzzz . . .

His weird
talent had
been the
cause of his
wife's **daddy's**
death.
Would it **home**
now take his
daughter's
life as
well?

TOM MOORE STARED AT HIS DESK,

which was piled high with top secret government files, profiles of the world's most threatening terrorist groups, and all other manner of classified information. At this moment, though, the most important document on it was the unfinished letter to his daughter.

Father Knows Best

> *Dearest Gaia,*
>   *I was closer to you Saturday night than I've been in years. Close enough to be reminded that you have my eyes, your mother's nose, and our combined determination.*
>   *Close enough to see you nearly shot.*
>   *Close enough to save your life.*

The pen trembled in his hand. Thank God he'd been there. His bullet had only hit the punk's shoulder, but it had been enough. For the moment, at least. Gaia had gotten away. Maybe the bullet had sent a message: Back off. Stand down. Give up. Tom could only hope. And anyway, there were other dangers stalking Gaia—ones far more grave, far less predictable.

One, he knew, was a sick son of a bitch with

whom, forty-some-odd years ago, Tom had shared a womb.

The thought made him physically ill. His brother. His twin brother. A deadly psychopath with a vendetta against Tom. Loki. Tom knew the name from the research his outfit provided. But he would have known it, anyway.

When they were children, his brother had fixated on the idea of Loki, the Norse god. A Satan-like hero, consumed by darkness and evil. It was no wonder that as an adult, he would adopt this moniker, under which to pursue his hateful purpose.

Tom said the word out loud. "Loki." It literally stung his vocal cords.

But what about his own name, his undercover name? Enigma, they called him. Definition: anything that arouses curiosity or perplexes because it is unexplained, inexplicable, or secret.

He gave a humorless laugh. Yes. That I am, he thought. I am a secret to my own child.

The name was dead-on. Tom Moore was an enigma, even to himself. He had been from childhood, when his remarkable talent had begun to make itself known. Why was he able to think the way he did? Why was he capable of solving the unsolvable? Why could his brain take in seemingly random patterns of words and numbers and make sense of them?

He could decode, decipher, predict, and presume with terrifying accuracy.

In high school he'd discovered, much to his amusement, that he could open any combination lock in the building. Handy for dropping little love notes into the lockers of cute girls (his buddy Steve's idea, and favorite pastime). But even now, so many years later, he still wanted to know why he could work codes and riddles so easily. Not *how*. He didn't care how, but how *come?* Why should this responsibility have fallen to him?

And it was such an awesome responsibility. He had no formal, written job description. In fact, as far as he knew, there was not a shred of printed information on him anywhere. But in his own mind he'd boiled his job description down to one sentence: Save the world.

Perhaps it was better that this ability had wound itself into the double helix of his DNA instead of his twin brother's. At least, Tom told himself, he used his skill for good. If Loki had been born with such a knack . . . Tom shuddered to think about it. Genetic predisposition was a freaky thing.

Gaia, for example. Her body chemistry was a source of even greater astonishment. It was as if the gods had said, "Let's give her brains, and beauty, and charm, and grace, and physical strength, but hold the fear. No use mucking up the gene pool with that useful emotion."

Again, why?

Tom let out a long rush of breath, expelling the question with the air in his lungs. He'd wondered too hard, too long on that one. Ironic: The only other conundrum besides himself that he couldn't solve was his own daughter.

So instead, he hid from her. And hid her, too.

Apparently not so well.

Because now Loki had her in his sights. And that filthy little street punk, whose ignorance was surpassed only by his willingness to hate, was stalking her.

Tom looked down at the unfinished letter, ran his finger over the greeting.

Dearest Gaia,

His talent had been the cause of his wife's death. Would it now take his daughter's life as well?

Not while there was breath left in his body, he vowed to himself.

He picked up his pen, hesitated, then added another line to the letter.

Daddy's home.

Then, as he did with every other note, letter, and card he'd written to Gaia over the last five years, he stuffed it into a file drawer and locked it away.

Not sending it was hard.

But sending it would make things so much harder.

KUDOS ON THE SUCCESSFUL COMPLE-
*tion of Test One. You are now to
commit an act of theft—a very spe-
cific act. George Niven has a computer disk that is of interest to us.
You will find this disk and drop it
off in Washington Square Park.
There will be a man there to receive
it. He will be disguised as a homeless man and he will
have a cart. Bring the disk to him, Gaia, and do it fast.
Time, after all, stops for no man. Not even for Sam . . .*

Slipping a Disk

"They want me to steal from George," Gaia said,
tearing her eyes from the note.

"Huh?" Ed blurted, following along as Gaia hurried
down the hall, second period completely forgotten.

"What do they want one of George's disks for?"
Gaia wondered aloud. She'd practically forgotten Ed
was there. George used to be a Green Beret with her
dad, and they'd been in the CIA together. Were the
kidnappers somehow connected to the government?

Oh, shit. Maybe George still had connections.
Maybe he had nude photos on someone in the
Pentagon. Or maybe the disk simply contained his
recipe for barbecue sauce, and this was just another
sham test, to get her to prove she was in this 100
percent.

But what if it wasn't barbecue sauce? It was

possible. After all, she'd sensed that George had always known where her father was. He never said anything; it was just this gut feeling she had. And now that her dad was back in town . . .

Could something terrorist-related be going down in Washington Square Park? Something involving CJ and the late Marco, and all those other small-time white-supremacist swine?

And what did any of this have to do with Sam? Why hadn't they just taken her?

If only they had just taken her.

"Gaia, have you heard a word I said?" Ed's voice suddenly broke through her stream of consciousness.

"No," she answered, unfazed.

"Well, I was just wondering if we're forgetting about school for the day, since you seem to be heading for the exit," Ed said.

Gaia stopped as the automatic door swung open with a loud buzz. "I think you should stay here," she said, glancing briefly at Ed's wide brown eyes.

"No way," Ed said determinedly. "This is no time to become Independent Girl." He pushed his way through the door and out onto the street. Fortunately, the school administration was a tad lax about keeping an eye on the handicap exits.

"Ed, I'm not *becoming* anything," Gaia said, stomping after him. A brisk October wind caught her hair and whipped it back from her face. "I just don't want you involved."

"I'm already involved," Ed said, staring straight ahead.

"Ed—"

"Gaia."

The tone of his voice made her pause. She might as well let him come home with her. She'd derail his efforts then. Somehow. She couldn't have him out on the street with her, where he was an easy target.

"Fine," she said, unwilling to let him get the last word. "But stay out of my way." She sidestepped past him and walked a few feet ahead, making sure to keep up a fast pace.

Gaia and Ed were halfway to George and Ella's house before either one of them spoke. Actually, she would have liked his advice, but how could she ask for it?

A) That would make her look needy, and she'd rather be dead than needy.

And

B) He didn't have all the facts.

As far as Ed could assume, George's computer files were most likely limited to bank statements and hints on preparing tangy marinades. He didn't know about George's past, which might in fact turn out to be continuing on into his present.

The question: Was Gaia willing to turn over one computer disk, which might, perhaps (and that was one gigantic perhaps there), contain a bunch of classified government crap that could help some terrorist destroy the world?

Or could she just let Sam die?

"So . . . does this disk or file or whatever have a name?" Ed asked finally. "Maybe it'll give you some clue about what it is."

Loyal *and* smart, that was Ed. Gaia scanned the remainder of the note and found the name.

And stopped in her tracks.

The file was called Scaredy Cat.

ELLA HAD LEFT A NOTE. OBVIOUSLY

No Warrant

Gaia had overlooked it in the commotion of the morning.

She found it on the hall table when she barreled in.

Surprised George with a day trip to the country. We won't be home until late. Ella.

"Finally," said Ed. "Something goes your way."

"Lucky me," Gaia responded, crumpling the note and tossing it over her shoulder as she tore through the house toward George's office. The stupid note reeked of Ella's perfume—some one-of-a-kind, New Age concoction she paid an arm and a leg for. Some freaky witchlike person in Soho produced it exclusively for her. It smelled like dead roses on fire and it made Gaia gag.

Gaia headed straight for the disk organizer on George's desk and quickly flipped through the contents. Nothing promising.

Like there was really going to be a disk marked Scaredy Cat in big red letters. Like anything could be that easy. Gaia pulled out a drawer and dumped the contents on the desk. Papers flew everywhere, and pencils, paper clips, and tacks scattered across the smooth wooden surface. A pair of worry beads hit the floor and rolled noisily into the corner.

"George is gonna love that," Ed said, wheeling into the room.

"Somehow neatness isn't my number one priority at the moment," Gaia said, rooting around in the mess. Again, nothing. Gaia groaned in frustration and went for the file cabinet.

Ed hit a key on the computer keyboard, reviving the machine from sleep mode. "Listen," he said, not taking his eyes off the screen, "I've become pretty proficient on this little modern convenience lately. I mean, until Arthur Murray comes up with swing lessons for paraplegics, there aren't a whole hell of a lot of ways for me to kill time."

Gaia didn't want to laugh, but for his sake she forced a smile.

"So I'm gonna hack around for a while and see if I can figure out who sent that e-mail," Ed said as the computer whirred to life.

"That's great," Gaia said absently. Great was an overstatement, but Ed locked up in George's office was a lot safer than Ed out on the street with some psycho kidnapper running around.

Gaia quickly leafed through files with yuppie titles like "IRS 1994" and "Appliance Warranties." She slammed the drawer so hard a framed certificate fell off the wall and clattered to the floor.

"Gaia, you're scaring me," Ed said.

"This is taking too long," she said, bringing her hand to her forehead and scanning the room for possible hiding places.

How many tests had the kidnappers set up? What if she didn't have time to complete them all? That disk could be anywhere. His briefcase. His underwear drawer. A safe-deposit box at some random bank. It could be with George in the country, for all she knew.

She glanced at the captain's clock on the wall. There was no time.

Gaia slammed her fist into the file cabinet. It didn't hurt nearly enough. But it did knock down a picture of Ella.

The picture clattered facedown on the desk. Gaia studied it for a moment. Pay dirt.

The front part of the frame wasn't sitting flush against the backing. It was bulging slightly, and there was a gap between the two parts. Gaia turned it sideways, gave one good shake, and the next thing she knew, she was holding several floppies, one of which was labeled Scaredy Cat. God, what a lucky break.

"I'm outta here," she said, grabbing her bag.

"Wait!"

But she couldn't wait. If she waited, she might have time to think about the fact that someone out there wanted information on her. Her. Not some secret government stash of anthrax or the plans to the Pentagon.

Her.

Gaia Moore.

And Sam might die because of it.

She wasn't waiting around to think about that.

You've got a
nice ass,
for an
angel.

not a perfect world

CJ LEANED AGAINST THE OUTER

wall of the arch that led into the park. He liked that arch. It was this big, beautiful thing— a knockoff of some bigger one from . . . where? France, maybe. He'd probably know if he hadn't quit going to school.

One Daydream

Who cared what it was called, anyway? He just liked it. He liked to look at beautiful things.

Like her.

Weird. He hated her. But man, he had some pretty crazy fantasies about her. She pulled him. All that strength and power wrapped up in all that soft sexiness. It gnawed at something in him.

Sometimes he thought about killing her.

Sometimes he just thought about her.

There was one daydream in particular he returned to over and over. In it, he'd be chasing her through the park, and she'd be totally freaked-out scared, and he'd grab her from behind—rough, but not enough to do any real damage. Maybe just a small bruise. A lasting ache.

And he'd spin her around and her hair would get all tangled up in his fingers.

Then she'd look up at him with those intense eyes, those sky-colored eyes, and she'd start begging.

First just begging him not to kill her, but then it would change.

She'd be begging him to kiss her.

And damn, he'd kiss her right. And then . . . then she'd love him. And he'd have the power. All of it.

But CJ knew better. He knew to put hate in front of love every time. That was the way it was with him and his boys. Hate put you in control, but love controlled you. So he let his mind slither back to hating her.

And then, as if he'd conjured her, she was there.

Sun in her hair. And that body. Those lips . . . on his lips.

Shit! Enough of this bullshit. He had to breathe deep. Once. Twice. Steady. He had to remind himself that the one thing he wanted to do more than kiss her was kill her. He *needed* to kill her if he wanted to stay alive himself.

He adjusted the sling on his arm. The other asshole he wanted to kill was whoever the hell had shot at him Saturday night.

The bullet had punctured his biceps, and damn, it had hurt. Still hurt. One of his boys had cleaned it out and given CJ the sling. Can't go to the hospital with a gunshot wound. They report it to the cops.

But CJ was sure it had hurt even more when Tarick had twisted it that morning. That wasn't a pain CJ was going to forget anytime soon. And it was all because of the bitch.

CJ focused on Gaia.

She paused, tilting her chin in his direction, like maybe she could hear him thinking about her. His heart thunked in his chest. His hand clenched into a fist. But she didn't see him. She kept walking.

Why wasn't she in school? This chick was damned unpredictable.

He watched her walk for a moment, liking the way her hips moved, `imagining kicking her hard in the stomach.` In some remote recess of his mind, he knew this made him a damn sick dude. In the one remaining brain cell that could still tell good from bad, he understood his thinking was damaged.

But he'd turned on the world, and right now she was his closest target.

OKAY, NOW *THIS* WAS A PROBLEM.

There were, on this crisp October morning, eight—count 'em, eight—homeless people by the fountain in Washington Square Park. And five of them were the proud owners of shopping carts.

Why hadn't the kidnapper foreseen this possibility?

Maybe he had. Maybe he just needed a little comic relief, and watching Gaia try to find the correct one was it. Will the real undercover operative for Sam's crazed kidnapper please stand up?

Well, at least she was able to eliminate the three cartless ones right off the bat. That left only five derelicts from which to choose.

The note had said a homeless *man*, hadn't it? Yes, it had. So the two bag ladies were out of the running.

Three remaining contestants. Gaia would need a closer look.

She clutched the disk in her pocket. She should have copied it. But Ed was at the computer, and if the files really were about her, there was no way she could let him see the contents. It would have taken too long to get him out of there, get everything copied, and clear off the hard drive.

Too much time away from the task at hand. Saving Sam.

She approached the first homeless man—a guy who appeared disconcertingly young to her. Thirty-eight, thirty-nine years old at the most. In a perfect world, he'd be walking his kid to kindergarten right now, grabbing a cab to his corner office on Wall Street, making the upright decision not to sleep with his secretary.

But this was not a perfect world, this was New York. And the guy was rooting through a trash can in search of his breakfast.

"Excuse me . . ."

He kept digging.

Gaia stepped forward. She could smell him now, ripe with his own humanity.

"Excuse me."

The guy whirled. "Get the hell away from me, bitch!"

Well, that was uncalled-for. So much for charity. She frowned at him. "I'm supposed to—"

"This is *my* trash can," he thundered, shaking a half-eaten apple at her. "Mine! So go 'way. Go on! Get out! Mine!" He bit the apple, then placed it inside a filthy old tennis shoe in his shopping cart (presumably to snack on later).

Yummy. Next?

Gaia made her way toward a slumped figure sitting on the ground. A crudely printed cardboard sign propped up in his lap read Desert Storm Veteran.

Well, that didn't take long, Gaia mused grimly. The Gulf War took place—what? Seven, eight years ago? She would have imagined it took at least a whole decade for one's life to fall apart so completely.

Gaia approached him, then bent forward and whispered, "Are you . . . looking for me?"

The guy looked up at her. "Yes," he said.

Thank God. Gaia reached into the pocket of her jacket for the disk. She drew it out, then hesitated. How could she be sure this was the guy?

"Yes," the man said again. "I am looking for you!" He reached out and grabbed Gaia's hand, wrenching the disk from her grasp with his grimy fingers.

Please tell me this is the right guy, she pleaded to herself silently. He grabbed the disk for a reason, right?

"I've been looking for you for a long time," the guy said. "You're the angel of the Lord, ain'tcha?"

And the reason was . . . he was totally in- sane.

Oh, shit.

"You've come to take me on to the Promised Land. I knew it the minute I saw that hair. That's the hair of an angel, all right. Only the Almighty Himself makes that color hair."

"Yeah. The Almighty and L'Oréal," Gaia snapped. She leaned down toward him. "Give me back the disk."

"No!" he shouted, clutching the floppy. "You've come to save me!"

"No. I've come to save Sam."

"So call me Sam." He was full of logic. "Just bring me on to heaven. Lead me there, angel. Take me."

"Believe me, mister, if *I* brought you to heaven, we'd most likely get jumped on the way." Gaia made a grab for the disk, but the guy was quick. He stuffed it into his grubby shirt.

"Give it to me," she demanded evenly.

"No! Not until you bring me to meet my Maker."

Gaia was starting to see red. Oh, he was going to meet his Maker, all right. He just wasn't going to like the method by which Gaia would send him there.

She pressed her fingers to her temples in frustration, demanding some patience from herself. She didn't want to have to pound the guy. He was already so pathetic as it was. She glanced around the park, hoping for inspiration, and found it.

"Okay," she said at last. "I'll bring you to meet your Maker. But if I do, you have to give me back my disk. Deal?"

The man nodded.

Gaia helped him up and started walking. He followed.

"Hey. You've got a nice ass for an angel."

Gaia almost laughed in disbelief. How could she have come to this? If her situation hadn't been so totally dire, she would have allowed herself a long, cathartic laugh. "The Lord's a real stickler for fitness," she muttered.

Gaia led him straight to one of the homeless people she'd eliminated in the first round. He was taller than her Desert Storm vet, with long, flowing gray hair and mismatched sneakers. "There he is," she said, pointing.

"That guy? In the ripped-up overcoat? That's God?"

Gaia nodded, hating to lie even under these circumstances. Hadn't somebody once said there's a little bit of God in every one of us?

"He don't even have a cart!" Gaia's companion was incredulous.

"Go figure."

The man scowled at her. "Listen, angel, you better not be shittin' me."

"Angels don't shit people." That much had to be true.

"He's drinkin' whiskey."

"Yeah, well . . ." Gaia shrugged. "He's been under a lot of pressure lately."

The homeless man hesitated, then reached into his shirt and withdrew the disk. Gaia snatched it before he could change his mind. She was about to run, but he spoke, and the emotion in his voice pinned her to her place. "Thank you, angel."

Gaia swallowed hard. "No sweat."

She took off for the fountain, putting her conscience on ice.

Her real contact was seated on a bench near it. She was beyond irritated at herself for not noticing the obvious signs before. So much for maintaining her wits.

The guy was straight from central casting, with his dirt-streaked face half hidden beneath a tattered hat, the shabby clothes, the wire shopping cart filled with trash bags and empty cans. What differentiated him from the others was that, unlike "God" with his mismatched sneakers, this guy was wearing a brand-spanking-new pair of expensive lug-soled boots.

Gaia approached him, feeling hollow. This man was one of the kidnappers. This man was in some way responsible for what was happening to Sam. He or someone he knew had inflicted pain on the person she loved.

She could have killed him, but that might get Sam killed.

There was no choice. For now she would do as they said. She wouldn't ask questions.

She reached into her pocket and withdrew the floppy disk, keeping her eyes firmly fixed on the visible lower half of the man's face. There was nothing recognizable. She memorized every detail in case she needed it later.

Cleft in the chin. Small scar on the jaw. Patchy stubble. Dark complexion.

Gaia moved closer, ready for even the slightest movement on his part. But he remained motionless, seemingly unaware of her.

She stepped up to the cart, dropped the disk into it, then turned to walk away.

"Tkduhplstkbg," the guy mumbled.

She stopped. "What?"

"Plastic bag. Take it."

Gaia squinted against the bright sunshine. On the handle of the shopping cart hung a small plastic bag from a Duane Reade drugstore. She reached for it cautiously. It was heavy.

She recognized the weight, and a surge of disgust filled her.

"No," she said.

The man lifted his eyes to her and glared. "Take it."

Gaia felt her free hand clench into a tight fist. One nice solid jab to the bridge of his nose and this guy would wake up in the next zip code.

But she couldn't. She had to think of Sam.

So she took the bag with the gun in it.

STREET SONG
for Her

Sidewalk sweet, she stands alone
In night and streetlamp
While the world sweats summer and
sirens sing
And hate pours down from the city sky
like a wicked rain,
it wets us all
until we're soaked with anger,
and fear enough
to make friends of enemies
and choices that burn like the heat
like the blades, like the bullets
like the broken promise
that I make
Even as I watch her where she stands
two steps from evil
one step from me
But in this world
You walk with danger
or you walk
alone.

He could see the slim silhouette of a switchblade in the

what the hell is this?

punk's back pocket.

GAIA SAT ON THE EDGE OF THE
fountain and placed the bag between her knees. She stuck one
hand in, letting her fingers
brush the butt of the gun for a
moment before fitting her palm
around it. It felt dead and
weighty.

Partners in Crime

And familiar.

Gaia hated guns. But she knew how to use them.

Her father had taught her marksmanship. While
other daddies were taking their nine-year-old
daughters to toy stores and ice cream parlors, Tom
Moore was bringing Gaia to the firing range, or far
into the woods with a rifle and a rusty tin can for a
target.

And she'd been a natural. From the start, she'd
rarely missed, and by the time her father had finished
training her, she didn't miss at all. Even
now, years away from the experience, she could still
hear the report of her last shot in the forest behind
their home. The deafening explosion of the shotgun,
the distant screaming *ping* of the bullet hitting the
can.

It blended in her memory with another explosion
and another scream.

Instinctively she let go of the gun. She pressed her
fingers against her eyes to make the memory go away.

80

Think of Sam. Think of him.

She fished around inside the bag, in case there was something else. There was.

A note.

"Of course." Gaia withdrew the note and read it.

Within the next twenty minutes, you will commit a crime. You may choose your victim, but you are to limit your territory to this park.

"My territory?" Gaia snarled.

You are not to go easy on this victim. The enclosed is to assist you in this task. You will also be required to enlist the assistance of a young man named . . .

Gaia felt the presence beside her at the exact second she read the name.

Renny.

She looked up and blinked. Renny was standing there, staring at her. This kidnapper had some major timing going on.

"Did I scare you?" he asked, taking a small step back.

"Not quite," she said.

He swallowed, gulped.

"Please tell me you're done with those skinhead assholes," Gaia said, looking Renny hard in the eyes, her mind leaping from one suspicion to the next.

"I am." Renny looked down at his sneakers. "But it's not that easy," he murmured. "You try living on the streets without anybody to watch your back."

"You don't live on the streets," Gaia said.

He met her gaze, his eyes almost black. "I don't *sleep* on the streets, Gaia. But I live here."

She considered his reasoning. It was true. Renny had nowhere else to go. From the sorry state of his clothes and the random bruises he was always sporting, home seemed less than appealing. So he lived for this park, those chess tables. And in how many places would a thirteen-year-old Hispanic poet be accepted? She sighed, remembering some of the verses he'd recited to her. That edgy, soulful poetry of his made her feel as though he'd scraped the words up off the sidewalk and strung them together into something that sang.

He straightened his shirt with his still small, wiry hands. Sometimes his obvious frailty pained Gaia—especially when he was trying to act tough.

She put her thumb beneath his chin and nudged it upward, so that he was looking her in the eyes. "Who sent you here?"

He shrugged.

"Don't bullshit me, Renny. This is important. Whoever sent me this . . ." She held up the bag, noting the sincerely puzzled expression in his eyes. "You really don't know?"

He shook his head hard—a childlike gesture. It made her heart feel empty.

"Tell me what happened."

He sat down on the rim of the fountain and leaned forward to rest his elbows on his knees. "I got a phone call at home."

"What were you doing at home on a Monday morning?" Gaia asked, trying to sound stern. She could barely pull it off.

"I go home for lunch sometimes," he said, shrugging. She narrowed her eyes at him. "Hey, you're not in school, either."

The boy had a point.

"Go on," Gaia said.

Renny took a deep breath. "Guy says, 'Go to the fountain in the park.' So I go."

"Did he threaten you?"

Renny gave her a lopsided grin. "Not really. 'Cept his voice sounded like he ate nails for breakfast, so I figure it's better if I do what he says."

Gaia was about to ask if the nail-eating voice had mentioned Sam, then thought better of it. The less Renny knew, the less danger he'd be in—relatively speaking, anyway. If the kidnapper knew his name, not to mention his phone number, he was already in this up to his eyeballs, based merely on the fact that he was associated with her.

"We have to pass a test," she said softly.

"A test?" He whistled low. "That doesn't sound good. That's what the guys told me just before they handed me that pistol to point in your face."

Gaia considered inquiring as to what sort of punishment Renny had faced in the wake of failing that test, but decided against it. She didn't think she could handle that at the moment.

"We have to, uh, commit a crime."

His big eyes got bigger. He said nothing.

"Something random. Something sort of rough." She held up the bag. "There's a gun in here."

"Damn."

"Yeah, damn," she said, staring across the park at a couple of fighting pigeons. "We've got to do it here. Now."

Renny mulled this over for a minute or so. "Why?"

"I don't want to tell you. Just trust me. If we don't . . ." She finished with a shrug.

"I'm in," he said.

Gaia nodded. She wasn't sure if that was good news or bad news. She had to think, to figure out the best way to go about this. Maybe there was a way to make the crime look real without actually harming anyone. She did know there was no way in hell she was going to fire that gun. She'd wield it, swing it around at whomever she ultimately chose to hassle, but she would not pull the trigger. The kidnapper would just have to settle for that.

Her eyes roamed the park, landing finally on the chess tables.

And there he was.

She recognized him immediately. The sleazebag. The well-dressed, self-important slimeball she'd played once—and only once, because he kept grabbing her thigh under the chess table. His name was Frank, she believed. He was about forty-seven, forty-eight years old but looked at least sixty with all his wrinkles. Tanning-salon regular, diamond pinky ring, woven loafers, even in October.

Jerk.

Gaia despised him. He'd hustled Zolov once, taking advantage of one of the sweet old guy's less lucid moments. Gaia figured Frank had walked away with Zolov's entire Social Security check that day, then used it to pay Lianne.

Lianne. Another pathetic story. Lianne was fourteen and a prostitute. Gaia was repulsed by her, but somewhere in her heart she felt sorry for her, too. The girl must have had one horrifying life to resort to turning tricks. And Frank was her best customer. Illegal, and disgusting.

The more Gaia thought about it, the more she decided she wouldn't entirely loathe roughing up Frank.

All she could hope was that wherever the kidnapper was watching from was far away enough to make Frank look like an innocent citizen, undeserving of Gaia's attack.

Without a word, she stood and made her way toward the chess tables.

Without a word, Renny got up and followed her.

TOM WIPED HIS GLASSES ON THE

inside of his shirt, then replaced them on the bridge of his nose. He was dressed blandly, in khakis and a denim shirt. Over his reddish blond curls he wore a suede baseball cap in dusty **Downright Nervous**

blue. The brim was tugged low on his brow.

He was invisible, leaning there against the tree. Watching.

Watching as his daughter strode purposefully away from the fountain. There was a scrawny kid with dark hair and golden skin tagging along with her.

But what was in the bag?

He lifted the brim of his cap a fraction of an inch and squinted at the plastic bag she was clutching. His heart took a nosedive when he realized what was in it. The outline of the object bulged unmistakably against the red-and-blue lettering of the pharmacy's logo.

Unmistakable to him, at least. Tom sent up a silent prayer thanking the gods for the indifference of New Yorkers. They would probably not even notice the girl, let alone the bag, let alone its contents.

She leaned down and whispered something to the kid. Pointed to the bushes. The kid nodded and they kept walking.

He kept his eyes trained on her as she crossed to the chess tables. A small, sad smile kicked up the edges of his mouth. Chess. His favorite game. And Gaia's. The first time she'd beaten him, she'd been only eight.

Tom stepped away from the tree for a better view, looking utterly preoccupied with nothing in particular, but seeing, feeling, every step she took.

She was approaching a middle-aged guy in an ugly designer suit who was seated on the losing side of a chessboard.

The kid looked a little jumpy. This bothered Tom. Street kids didn't get jumpy without a good reason. And this kid looked downright nervous. Maybe even scared.

Gaia didn't look scared. Gaia never looked scared.

What she looked, lifting the bag and pressing it to the shoulder of the ugly suit, was determined. Tom moved away from the tree.

Why was she doing this? Had his leaving poisoned her so badly that she'd taken up petty crime? Or was there more to it?

Of course there was. He knew that was the real burden of the life he'd given her: For Gaia, nothing would ever be exactly as it appeared. Nothing would ever be simple. There would always be layers, dimensions, motives, and questions. And horrible choices.

But why was she choosing this? What had brought her here? Had her confusion and loneliness made her an easy mark for a gang? Had his absence led her to join one? Had she, in search of something resembling a "family," been sucked into their evil world?

No. Not Gaia. The girl was smart and, he knew, good. Good at her core, good in her very essence.

This was something bigger. More dangerous. Something enormous must have been at stake. And clearly her sense of urgency was overshadowing her good judgment.

This was not robbery for robbery's sake.

But it was still robbery.

Tom had to stop her, but how? Could he create some kind of distraction—knock over a homeless guy's cart, perhaps? Draw her attention away from what she was about to do, long enough to bring her back to her senses?

He took two long strides in her direction, then stopped cold.

The punk. The punk he'd shot at the other night. His arm was in a sling, and he was running toward Gaia.

Tom shuddered. He could see the slim silhouette of a switchblade in the punk's back pocket.

He meant business.

Tom should have rid the world of this menace Saturday night, when he'd had the chance. But Tom had let his emotions affect his accuracy. He'd missed his opportunity.

And now his hands were tied. This was a crowded park, in broad daylight. So for the moment, much to Tom's revulsion, CJ would have to be allowed to live.

Tom wondered what Gaia had done to piss CJ off. Maybe the kid had come on to Gaia once, and she'd blown him off. With a creep like CJ, a broken heart could easily become a fatal attraction.

There were only two things Tom knew for sure. One was that for the second time in less than forty-eight hours, he was going to have to put himself between Gaia and death. The other was that he was willing to do it.

FRANK LOOKED UP FROM HIS NEAR-

Your Money or Your Life

defeat on the chessboard and raised one bushy eyebrow at Gaia. "What the hell is this?"

Gaia, her hand on the gun inside the bag, pushed the barrel harder into his shoulder. "*This* is a gun," she told him in a matter-of-fact voice. "Let's go somewhere a little more private."

"Oh, for Christ's sake."

Renny took off for the bushes that lined the east side of the park. "Follow the kid," Gaia said. Frank just stared at her, wide-eyed.

"Let's go," said Gaia, cocking the hammer.

"Jeez! Hey. Jeez!" Frank wriggled up from his seat and slowly followed Renny. His opponent, for obvious reasons, got up and fled. Two people at a table nearby scooted farther away. Gaia didn't have much time.

She shoved Frank in the back so he would hurry up, and he ducked behind the bushes. Gaia could only hope that the all-knowing kidnapper could see them back here and wouldn't miss her command performance.

Renny went to the edge of the bushes to keep watch, and Gaia grabbed Frank by the back of his collar, jerking him around to face her. He swore, swatting at her like a `cartoon boxer,` managing to clip her on the chin. She released him, used the hand that wasn't holding the gun to slap his face, then grabbed a handful of his greasy hair and pulled him to her.

"Didn't your mother ever teach you not to hit girls?" she asked, her nose practically touching his. He smelled like bourbon and chewing tobacco. Gaia had to struggle to keep from hurling.

Renny turned from his post. "Give us your wallet," he demanded in a forceful voice that sounded like it came from someone much bigger and older.

"You're supposed to be keeping watch," Gaia spat out. Renny turned around again.

"Give us your wallet," Gaia echoed.

"Yeah. Yeah, sure." Frank shoved a trembling hand into his breast pocket, withdrew a fat billfold, and slowly offered it to Gaia. For a moment it just sort of hung there between them, off the tips of his fingers.

It was almost too easy. Gaia had a feeling the kidnapper had been hoping for a bit more drama. The asshole had thought this out well. Do this too quickly and easily, and the kidnapper probably wouldn't be satisfied.

Take too long and she'd end up stuck in jail.

And Sam would die.

Gaia swallowed hard and narrowed her eyes at Frank. "Look petrified," she ordered. "Cry."

Sweat poured from his temples down his cheeks. "What, are you kiddin' me?"

"Does it look like I'm kidding?"

He gave a nervous laugh. "No, sweetheart. It don't."

His use of the word *sweetheart* nearly caused her to

slap him again. "Cry," she repeated dryly, casually lifting her knee into his groin.

"Uhhnnffff!" Frank doubled over. "You little . . ."

"I don't see any tears," Gaia hissed, taking hold of his fleshy neck and applying a firm grip to the pressure point.

"Ahhh . . ." Frank's face contorted in pain, then he let out a satisfactory sob.

Gaia didn't let go. "No more sharking Zolov or anybody else," she commanded fiercely from above.

"Yeah," moaned Frank. "Yeah. Okay."

"Gaia?" Renny said tentatively. "I think we have to go."

She let go of Frank's neck and took a small step backward. He straightened up cautiously and handed over his wallet.

"This never happened," she hissed.

To her surprise, Frank gave her a cold smile. "Aye, yo. You think I'm gonna tell anybody I got held up by two little shits like youse? A freakin' Rican who ain't got hair on his chest, and his partner, the prom queen?"

At that Gaia shoved the bagged pistol right under his chin. "You *ever* insult me like that again, and I'll kill you!"

Then she grabbed Renny and ran.

Prom queen, my ass.

CJ WAS HEADING TOWARD HER LIKE

Meanwhile, Back at the Arch . . .

a tiger running down a wounded gazelle.

Gaia had no idea, focused as she was on committing her felony. The guy in the ugly suit was doubled over.

But Tom's eyes were trained on the tiger. The tiger had his hand on the knife.

Tom sprang into action. He hurdled a park bench, dodged someone on skates, and connected with the tiger in a check that would have done Lawrence Taylor more than proud.

CJ hit the pavement.

Tom kept running.

And Gaia was gone.

THE COP SKIDDED UP TO THE CURB

Two Blocks Later . . .

and got out of the car as though he were auditioning for a walk-on in *NYPD Blue*.

"Hey! You two."

Damn.

Gaia could feel the change in Renny as he walked alongside her. He tensed, and his body temperature climbed at a rate that was actually detectable.

Fear, she thought. So those are the symptoms, huh? Her own body was cool, her heartbeat slow and steady. Even when faced with losing Sam, the guy who made the future seem worth living, still she didn't feel fear. She felt anger, determination, frustration. But no fear. If she couldn't feel fear for Sam, couldn't feel the heartrending, temperature-raising emotion that every other human being felt, could she really love him?

She was drifting. She had to focus. She had to make use of the capabilities she had, not mourn the one that was missing.

"Don't panic," she whispered to Renny. "They can smell it." Or so she'd heard.

"Young lady . . ."

Gaia turned and graced the cop with an innocent smile. "Were you talking to me, Officer?"

"Yes."

He was really young. It could have been his first day on the job. He had one of those square chins that was pretty much a prerequisite for joining the police force.

"Is something wrong?" Gaia asked. She made no

attempt to hide the plastic bag. Both the gun and Frank's wallet were still in it.

"I've just come from the park."

She looked suitably blank, patient. Renny, however, was bouncing, shifting his weight, preparing to split. She wished he'd just stand still.

"There was a mugging," the cop continued.

Gaia gasped. Nice touch. "Oh my God."

"Nothing too serious. Guy's wallet was stolen. Couple of eyewitnesses said it was two kids. Boy and a girl." He cleared his throat, an unspoken apology.

He hated this. Gaia could tell. A serious young law enforcement officer like him should have better things to do than hassle a couple of kids. Gaia could actually see him thinking this. She wasn't sure whether to be thankful for or repulsed by his obvious attraction to her. It might just get them out of this.

"Well, we didn't see anything," she said with a dainty shrug. "We weren't even in the park."

The cop nodded. "Why aren't you two in school?" he asked, as if it had just occurred to him.

"We're home-schooled." Gaia fired this out so quickly that even she believed it. "My mom teaches us." She put an arm around Renny's shoulder, pressing down ever so slightly, to get him to quit fidgeting. "This is my stepbrother."

Another nod from Glamour Cop. He hesitated, as if he might ask for their names, but didn't. He turned to get back in the car, then turned back.

"By the way, what's in the bag?"

"The bag? What's in the bag?" Gaia knew she sounded like an idiot, but the question had caught her off guard. She'd thought they were home free.

"What's in the bag?"

Nothing. Just a gun and a stolen wallet.

Then she heard Renny say, "Tampons."

It was all Gaia could do to keep from laughing out loud.

"Tampons," Renny repeated, snatching the bag from Gaia. He held it out to the cop, but his eyes were on Gaia. "I hope I got the right kind," he said in the most disarmingly innocent tone Gaia had ever heard from him—maybe from anyone. "Superabsorbent, you said, right? The deodorant kind?"

He turned his doe eyes back to the cop. "She gets embarrassed, see, so I go into the pharmacy and get 'em for her." He gave the bag a little shake. "Wanna check?"

The cop, looking embarrassed himself, shook his head. "No," he said with a slight croak. "Not necessary."

He ducked back into his car and drove off.

Gaia was gaping at Renny in disbelief. "Where'd you learn to lie like that?"

"I dunno." He threw her a crooked grin. "Home school, maybe?"

Gaia wanted to hug him, but of course she didn't. Instead she pressed her index finger forcefully into his chest. "Lying. Bad. Stealing. Worse. I only did this because somebody's life is in danger, and I had no other choice."

Renny opened his mouth, probably to ask whose life, but Gaia barreled right along.

"From now on, I want you to stay the hell away from that stupid gang. You don't need them to watch your back." She paused, hoping she could pull off the next sentence without sounding like a total Hallmark card. "You've got me, all right? I'll . . . watch your back."

She didn't wait around to see the expression on his face.

Media people who have a problem with rap music, controversial movies, or premarital sex like to throw around the term "family values."

I don't mind saying I don't even know what the hell they're talking about.

I mean, okay, I'm not an idiot. I *know* what they're talking about—two parents with college degrees, kids in clean sneakers, mass or service or temple (whichever is applicable) every weekend, meat loaf on Monday night, freshly cut grass, and a minivan. Yeah, I know what they mean.

I just don't know it from firsthand, personal experience. Anymore.

Consider my family, for example. My current one, that is. Absentee (big time) father, well-meaning concerned guardian, bitchy wife of guardian, chess geeks whose last names I don't even know. That, at present, is as close as I come to having a family.

Can you imagine this crowd sitting down to meat loaf and mashed potatoes some evening?

And what about Renny? He's been so brain-poisoned he actually thought he could purchase himself a family (of violent, hate-obsessed misfits) with a bullet to my face. What makes me ill is wondering how majorly screwed up the kid's real family must be in order for violent misfits to constitute an upgrade.

But the only family I can seem to think about right now is Sam's.

They've got to be somewhere in the realm of decent, don't they? Or else how could they have produced such a perfect human being as Sam?

All right, so he's not *perfect*—there's that 108-pound wart on his ass (you know her as Heather), and the guy's a master of the mixed signal. But if he's

not Mr. Perfect, he's certainly
Mr. Pretty Damn Close.

The thing that's turning me
inside out now is the fact that,
for all I know, his parents are
sending him a package of homemade
peanut butter cookies baked by
his little sister (for some reason, I imagine he has one), with
a note saying that Uncle Mort
says hi and they'll see him on
parents' weekend. Maybe they are
at this very second dialing his
number, calling him up just to
say hi, and since he's not answering, they'll simply assume
he's at the library, studying for
some huge exam.

Maybe they're eating meat loaf
and mashed potatoes, and com-
plaining that he only calls home
when he needs money.

But the point is, their son's
life is in danger and they have
absolutely no idea.

That's killing me.

I mean, okay, *my* life is in
danger and *my* father has

absolutely no idea. But somehow
that doesn't bother me as much as
Sam's family not knowing.

   I guess maybe because I'm fig-
uring if they knew, they'd actually care.

   Whereas if my father knew,
he'd have to stop and think to
remember who I was before he
could go back to whatever it is
that he's been doing all these
years and continue to not give a
shit.

It wasn't that she didn't want to pray for Sam. She just wasn't sure how.

she's no angel

IT DIDN'T MAKE SENSE.

Ella had dragged him all the way up to Greenwich, cooing and purring about some private time together, enjoying the romance of the countryside on an autumn morning.

Cozy in Connecticut

So what did she do the moment they arrived?

She dropped herself into a chair at the most Manhattan-like cafe she could find and ordered a double martini. At ten forty-five in the morning.

George ordered coffee for himself, then reached across the table and took her hand.

"This was a great idea," he said, hoping to divert her attention away from her drink. "You and me, the country . . ."

Ella nodded, glancing around the cafe.

"So what's on the agenda? Picnic on the Sound? A little sailing, perhaps?"

Ella sighed. "Oh, I don't know. Shopping, maybe."

"Shopping?" George raised an eyebrow. "Honey, you can shop anytime in New York. I thought the idea was to come up here and do something that involved grass and trees and quiet country lanes." He'd known when he married her that she wasn't exactly an outdoorswoman, but surely even the most pampered Manhattanite would be enchanted by the old-time New England charm of this town.

Ella wrinkled her nose. "Country lanes, George? Really."

"Sure. Me and you, the breeze, the sunshine. Some cozy little grotto somewhere . . ."

She looked as if she was considering it. "Well . . ." She sighed, lifting her dazzling eyes to his.

A wave of pure attraction washed over him. The truth of it was that he didn't really much care what they did, as long as they were together. He would try to talk her into doing something slightly more romantic than signing credit card receipts, but he wouldn't push. Whatever she wanted was, in all sincerity, fine with him.

So he was smitten with his own wife. So sue him.

The beverages came, and George let go of Ella's hand to allow the waiter to deliver her martini. When he reached for it again, she made a quick grab for the drink.

George sat back in his chair, telling himself she was just thirsty.

"What time is it?" she asked.

He checked his watch. "Close to eleven. Why?"

Ella lifted one shoulder in a shrug. "We'll take the two-thirty train back to Grand Central."

"Back?" George tore open a sugar packet and poured it into his coffee. "We just got here. Listen, there's supposed to be a beautiful little horse farm just a few towns away. I read about it in the travel section of the *Times*." He gave his wife what he hoped was an irresistible grin. "How about we shop this morning, then we can spend the afternoon cantering through some of those sprawling open fields we passed on the way into town?"

"Those weren't open fields. Those were people's yards."

He laughed. She didn't.

"C'mon. What do you say to a little horseback riding?"

She sighed again, causing her ample chest to swell against the satin of her blouse. "I'm not exactly dressed for riding," she said, then gently, seductively caught her lower lip between her teeth. "But if you really want to . . ."

She had him. And they both knew it.

"Shopping it is." George lifted the cup to his lips, tramping down the prickle of disappointment. A moment or two passed before he spoke again. "Have you noticed that Gaia's been acting a little distracted lately?"

"Distracted?" repeated Ella, as if she herself hadn't been paying attention. She looked over her husband's shoulder and out the window.

"I'm worried about her."

"Don't be." Ella traced the rim of her martini glass with one slender finger. "She's a teenager. They're a species unto themselves. What looks peculiar to us is perfectly normal for them."

"Normal, huh? Saturday night she came home sweating, panting, all out of breath—"

"Oh?" Ella pursed her lips in disdain. "Were you waiting up, George?"

"No. Well, not exactly. I just happened to be awake."

This time she did laugh. "And did you go to her? Ask her if all was well? Tuck her in?"

George shook his head. "Maybe I should have."

"She's seventeen!" Ella exclaimed in a patronizing tone. "And as far as the sweating and panting goes, well, that's exactly the kind of reaction a teenage girl would experience after spending hours teasing some poor boy in the backseat of his car!"

"C'mon, Ella," said George, his face flushing at her inference. "I don't think Gaia —"

"Oh, please! She's no angel, George, as much as you'd like to believe she is." Was it his imagination, or was there bitterness behind her voice?

"She's been through a lot," George said, eyeing his wife warily.

Ella rolled her eyes. "So you've said—often."

"I still think I should have talked to her the other night," George said, turning his profile to her and staring out the window. "She's lost so much." George had no idea what it was like to be a teenage girl. He could barely recall what it was like to be a teenage boy. But he knew what it was like to have someone he loved snatched away. He remembered that vividly.

"We're all she has," George said, finally turning back to Ella. "Maybe she's lonely—"

"Fine, George," said Ella, sighing. "Gaia's lonely. Not horny—just lonely. The point is, she probably would have told you to mind your own business, anyway." She paused, then said pointedly, "She's not our child."

At this George felt a familiar jolt—a longing. *Our child.* His, theirs, hers. His eyes searched Ella's questioningly.

"Oh, no." She held up her hand like a traffic cop and laughed again. "Don't even go there, George Niven. We've discussed it." Her other hand went to her `firm, flat tummy`. "This figure is not to be tampered with." She cleared her throat, then added, "Yet."

It was the most unconvincing "yet" he'd ever heard in his life. The waiter returned with more coffee for him and a fresh martini for Ella. Three olives this time, instead of two. Clearly he hadn't heard her remark about flat-tummy maintenance. Or maybe he just liked her.

They sipped their drinks without further conversation until the silence was interrupted by the bleating of her cell phone.

She flipped it open. "Yes?"

George watched her near-expressionless face as she listened. After almost two full minutes, she said, "Fine." Then she hung up.

"Who was that?"

"No one important," she said, plucking a plump olive from the toothpick in her glass.

George smiled teasingly. **"No one important who?"**

She looked at him. "If you must know, it was Toshi. My feng shui appointment has been canceled for tonight."

"Oh." George lowered his gaze to the table.

Toshi, huh? He wanted to believe her, but at the same time he had a very strong hunch that the call had had nothing to do with feng shui.

If Ella had any hunches regarding his hunch, she didn't show it.

She went right on drinking her martini.

And, he imagined, waiting impatiently for five fifteen.

GAIA STUFFED FRANK'S TACKY EEL-

Another West Side Story

skin wallet into the pocket of her faded sweatshirt jacket and shoved the gun into the bottom of the messenger bag. She took a deep breath and let it out slowly.

So she'd just conducted her first mugging.

It was not a good feeling. Gaia kicked at a crumpled-up McDonald's bag as she walked along the cracked sidewalk. She didn't like playing the part of a lowlife, even if the joke was on Frank.

But it was all about saving Sam. Gaia booted the bag into the sewer. The end justifying the means, and all that. Very `Machiavellian`.

So where was the next test? Once again she was left with downtime while Sam was sitting alone somewhere, suffering. Gaia felt her heart squeeze painfully as she remembered Sam's swollen face. She pressed her eyes closed, as if she could block out the image. Could she find fear—even a tiny shred of it—if she kept that image in her mind's eye?

This was torture. Maybe that was the point.

Trying to distract herself, she pulled out Frank's wallet again and flipped it open. There was a `stack of bills` inside, and Gaia pulled them out, counting quickly so that no street thugs would spot her and get any ideas. Three hundred and fifty bucks. Not bad. What the hell was she going to do with it?

When she looked up, Gaia noticed she had stopped right in front of St. Joseph's Church. That couldn't be a coincidence. She stuffed the money and wallet back into her pocket and ducked inside the church.

The place was perfectly quiet. There was no one in sight, and the sunlight streaming through the stained-glass windows revealed dancing particles of dust. Gaia found herself thinking how weird it was that all churches always smelled the same. Not that she'd been to very many—just enough to know they all had that same damp, smoky smell.

As Gaia wandered down the carpeted center aisle, she wondered how many times "Amen" and "Please, God" had been whispered in there. She got the feeling that if she listened carefully enough, she might hear the echoes.

It occurred to Gaia that if the kidnappers were still watching her closely, a deserted church would be the perfect place for them to attack. Gaia wished they would. It would be nice to get this over with. Kick some ass, find out where Sam was, get him, and then go the hell home. She was tired of this already.

There was an alcove toward the front of the church with a brass stand in it. On the stand were rows upon rows of stubby white candles in little glass holders, some red, some blue. Gaia smirked. Religious *and* patriotic.

Gaia knew what the candles were for. One night when she'd first moved in with George and Ella, she'd stayed up late, unable to sleep, and watched a rerun of *West Side Story* on TV. Natalie Wood, as Maria, had a little setup like this one with the candles and everything, right in her apartment. She was lighting candles and saying prayers.

Gaia went to the alcove and found what she was looking for—a worn wooden box with Donations painted painstakingly across the front. Gaia was pretty sure she was supposed to make a contribution before lighting a prayer candle. Someone had to pay for all that wax. Fine with her. She stuffed Frank's money into the box. She figured that $350 bought her the right to start a bonfire. But she wasn't exactly good with prayers. She wasn't even entirely sure of what religion she was supposed to practice. Her family was one big melting pot.

Next to the candles there were a bunch of skinny sticks, like extralong toothpicks, sticking out of a little pot of sand. The ends on some of them were charred.

Okay, I get it, she thought. You use a lit candle to light the stick, then use the stick to light your own candle.

She picked up one of the long, fragile sticks. Should she or shouldn't she?

Part of her felt like a serious hypocrite. But a bigger part of her felt she needed help from wherever she could get it.

She breathed in the church smell and thought about Sam. He didn't deserve this. No one deserved this. It was all her fault.

Then she poked the stick into the flame of one of the burning candles. What prayer went with that one?

112

she wondered. Had it been bigger than hers? Had it been answered?

She held the stick over an unlit candle and for a moment just watched the flame dance. Then, in spite of her $350 donation, she slammed the burning end of the stick into the sand and got out of there.

It wasn't that she didn't want to pray for Sam. She just wasn't sure how.

GAIA RAN ALL THE WAY HOME,

A New Video Release

hoping at every turn that she'd be stopped by another crazed fake homeless man with a note. No such luck.

She was ready to scream with frustration when she rounded the corner onto Perry Street and caught a glimpse of George and Ella's front stoop. There was a package. Time for a sprint. It seemed like forever before the box was in her hands, but the card had her name on it. And since she didn't belong to the Jam of the Month club or anything, she was pretty sure it was from her friendly neighborhood kidnapper.

She let herself inside (still no Ella, thank God) and took the stairs to her room in threes. After slamming her bedroom door and locking it behind her, Gaia pulled the Duane Reade bag out of her messenger bag and shoved it, gun and all, under her bed.

Then she tossed her messenger bag on her mattress, sat down at her desk, and opened the box. Wonderful. There was another video inside. And, of course, another note. This was getting old.

"Wonder what this movie's rated," Gaia muttered.

Gaia gathered up her stuff again and jogged back downstairs to the living room. She shoved the tape into the VCR and hit play.

Gaia's eyes narrowed as an image of her own face—so close up she could count her own pores—flickered onto the screen. The camera panned back to reveal her and Renny sitting by the fountain. She felt the blood start to rush through her veins, bringing an angry flush to her face.

Whoever had filmed this had been so close. How could she have missed him? How stupid was she?

Lowering herself onto the plush couch, Gaia watched as she and Renny crossed the park. It was like some kind of morbid home movie.

Isn't Gaia adorable, sticking that pistol into Frankie's shoulder, stealing his wallet, kneeing him in the groin?

She hit the off button, pulled the cassette out of

114

the slot, and proceeded to `tear its celluloid guts out`. After that, she did the same to the tape of Sam and Heather, which was still in her messenger bag. Then she unfolded the note that had come with the new tape, and read it.

Then she read it again.

Suddenly Gaia really wished she'd lit that candle.

You are doing surprisingly well. Your next test may not be so easy. Your friend in the wheelchair is to be your next victim. No violence is necessary. What we want is for you to HUMILIATE him. In public.

This humiliation, Gaia, is to be thorough. Uncompromised. You will emotionally destroy this young man.

And if you are wondering why . . . don't. You need no reason other than that I require you to do it.

IF YOU FAIL, SAM MOON WILL DIE.

TOP TEN WAYS TO EMBARRASS A
KID IN A WHEELCHAIR

10. Buy him a pogo stick.

9. Ask him how often he has to have his tires rotated.

8. Tell him you'd like to borrow his chair to guarantee yourself a good seat for *Cats*.

7. Attach a bumper sticker that reads Warning: I Break for Orthopedic Surgeons.

6. Totally fawn over him, and tell him how sorry you feel for him.

5. Totally ignore him and pretend he doesn't exist, like everybody else does.

4. One good shove down the handicap ramp.

3. Invite him to visit the top of the Statue of Liberty.

2. Ask him, "You must really feel like a loser during the national anthem, huh?"

1. Say something—anything—of a sexual nature, implying that it's not just his legs that are permanently limp.

I can't believe I am even capable of coming up with these things. It makes me sick. I make me sick.

How am I going to do this?

Why are they making me do this?

And then the
world went
surreal on
him. Because
Gaia was not
Gaia.

like

lox?

ED ROLLED HIS CHAIR OUT OF HIS

Seduction 101

eighth-period class and into the crowded hallway. He'd made it back to school in time for the chem exam, which, unfortunately, had been even more difficult than he'd expected. With all of the insanity running through his head, he'd be lucky to pull a C plus. Of course, in light of what was happening to Gaia and Heather, not to mention Sam, a C plus didn't sound too terrible.

The good news was that the morning's searching had yielded major information.

It was the noise. A noise he knew. Or used to know.

He'd sat there in George's study for over an hour, viewing the video e-mail of Sam over and over. Just as he was about to pack it in Ed had noticed a noise in the background. It had been there all along. He couldn't imagine how he'd missed it, unless his eyesight was shutting down from all the staring and his ears were taking over. But as soon as he detected it, he recognized it.

Wrrrzzzzzzzzz. Clank. Wrrzz.

It was a noise he himself had made for years. A noise he'd never make again.

And he knew there was only one place in New York

City where that noise could occur precisely the way it sounded in the background of the e-mail.

Wrrrzzzzzzzz. Clank. Wrrrzzzzzzzz . . .

"Ed, man! Totally nice ride. You got serious air on that one, dude. Is this the most bodacious ramp in the city or what? Let's see it again. Go for it!"

Wrrzz. Clank.

Yeah, Ed knew the noise.

He pushed aside the memory and gritted his teeth at the way the crowd in the hallway parted for him.

At least it meant getting to a private place to use his phone faster, although the chances of Gaia being home were slim to none. If the girl was going to insist on being the `reluctant superhero,` the least she could do was invest in a cell phone.

Ed rounded a corner, and there she was. Right in the middle of the jostling, locker-slamming crowd. No dialing necessary.

His smile was automatic. (Not to mention the reaction from a more southern portion of his anatomy.) He waved, `relishing` the way he could see her eyes burning like blue flames, even from this distance.

"Good news," he began, but the rest of his greeting caught in his windpipe. She was striding—no, more like stomping—in his direction. Panic engulfed him. What had happened? Had Sam been hurt? Worse thought: Had she?

She stopped about a foot in front of him.

And then the world went surreal on him. Because Gaia was not Gaia. Everything about her said hatred—the rigidity of her shoulders, the tightness of her face.

"Hey," she barked. Yes, barked. It was a horrible sound, one he couldn't reconcile with the sexy, slightly raspy voice he loved hearing over the phone every night.

He stared at her, peripherally aware that people were slowing down, glancing their way. They were curious, but not committed just yet. School was over, after all. There were soccer balls to dribble, lattes to drink, boyfriends to kiss.

"Hey . . . freak."

Okay, now she had their attention. Ed opened his mouth to say something but hadn't the slightest idea what that something should be. His eyes slid over her carefully. Was she bruised? No. Drugged? Didn't seem to be. Brainwashed? Not likely.

What was going on?

She said it again. "Hey, freak."

Ed wished he could make himself meet her gaze. "Something I can do for you?"

A strangled sound came out of her mouth. It took him a second to understand it was supposed to be laughter.

"I doubt it," she said. "In fact . . ."

He noted that her fists were clenching and unclenching.

"In fact, I doubt there's anything you can do for any girl in this school."

This earned her an "ooh" from the onlookers, and she let her eyes fall purposely to his midsection. Ed felt scalded by the heat of them. His heart hit the badly scuffed floor. She couldn't possibly have just said that.

"So am I right, Ed?" she prodded. "I mean, we all know you're paralyzed from the waist down, but I'm curious. Does *anything* still work?"

Horror filled him as she came closer. She placed one hand on each of his chair's armrests and smiled wickedly. "Aren't you going to tell me?" she asked in a seductive tone he might have liked under different circumstances. "Or am I going to have to find out for myself?"

This piece of cruelty was rewarded with another "ooh."

Ed's brain vaguely registered that not one single son of a bitch in the crowd was making an attempt to defend him. But he didn't actually care about them. He cared about her. Too much.

And she was destroying him. Why?

His voice decided to work without his permission, and he heard himself say, a bit pathetically, "You're enjoying this, aren't you?"

"Yes," she assured him, still smiling. "I like torturing you. About as much as I like lox."

Lox.

"Like lox?"

"Hate them."

His heart surged. This wasn't real. She was faking. He pulled his eyes to hers at last. And she answered him. It wasn't a word, or an action, or even an expression. It was something deeply unnameable in her eyes.

This was her next test. For some inexplicable purpose, the kidnapper wanted her to hurt him. So be it. He'd play along.

Unfortunately, one of the male spectators chose that moment to get righteous. He stepped forward and said, "Leave him alone."

Ed wouldn't have believed it, but in that second he could actually *see* her resolve falter. One word from a pseudo-Samaritan and she was ready to crumble—her belief in this heinous charade was that fragile.

He felt her begin to back away, and he knew he couldn't let her. Too much was riding on it. Sam's life. More important, possibly her safety.

So Ed lifted his chin. "You wanna know if it still works?"

She blinked, clearly taken aback by this reaction. He kept his eyes glued to hers. *Don't quit, Gaia. I understand. Don't back down.*

One corner of her mouth twitched.

"Yeah," she said, her reluctance audible only to him. "I wanna know if you're still man enough to do it."

"Well, that depends." Ed reached forward, catching

her around the waist and pulling her onto his lap. "Are you woman enough to make me want it?"

The crowd's "oohs" rose to a crescendo now, and the applause that erupted froze her.

"C'mon, Gaia," he urged, knowing she had to bring this full circle to satisfy the kidnappers. "Make me."

"Fine, I will."

"Fine. So do it."

"Fine."

She leaned toward him—somehow the movement was at once gentle and violent—until her mouth was dangerously close to his.

"Principal!"

Suddenly the crowd scattered like rats, leaving Ed unkissed and alone in the hall with Gaia, who was sitting sidesaddle across his thighs. Now that they were alone, she made a move to exit his lap, but didn't get far.

"I think maybe you should get off me now," Ed suggested calmly.

"I'm trying!" Gaia snapped in reply. The zipper on the outer pocket of her cargo pants was caught on his sweater, and she was struggling to disengage herself. "I promise you this is not what I want to be doing right now."

He chuckled. "Yeah, you just keep telling yourself that, Gaia."

Ed could hear the principal's footsteps approaching the corner of the deserted hallway. Gaia let out a little yelp of frustration.

"Scared?" he baited.

"Annoyed," she said. She let go of the zipper and met his eyes for a second. "And very sorry," she added under her breath. "Not scared."

She tried jerking her leg sideways, and wound up straddling him.

"We might want to wait until *after* the principal's come and gone," he said.

The sound of the principal's whistling floated toward them. "I really think you should get off me, Gaia."

"Hey, nobody told you to put me on your lap," Gaia said calmly. She stopped struggling. Was she just going to let them get caught like this?

"Well, nobody told you to seduce me in the middle of the hall!" Ed said, trying to push her off him. She really was stuck.

"As a matter of fact," she hissed, lowering her face to his until their noses were touching, "you're wrong. Somebody did."

Then came the principal's booming voice. "Mr. Fargo! What is the meaning of this?"

Suddenly his head contained more than its allotted share of blood. Ed toyed with the idea of making a joke—something about extra credit for biology class—but decided against it.

"Miss Moore, kindly remove yourself from Mr. Fargo's . . . er . . . lap."

"If you get me a scissors, that just might be possible," Gaia said.

Sarcasm. Ed closed his eyes. Good strategy, Gaia.

Principal Reegan gave them his patented I've-seen-it-all-already-so-don't-even-bother stare. "I'll inform Ms. Strahan that she can expect you both in the detention hall," he said. He turned on his heel and walked off.

"Good one, Gaia," Ed said with a sigh.

Gaia stared after Reegan. "Do you think that means he's not going to get me a scissors?"

Heather Gannis was nothing if not brave. **armor** She proved that every day, didn't she?

BY THE TIME GAIA AND ED ARRIVED

at the detention hall, Ed had a hole in his sweater, and Gaia had a chunk of blue cotton sticking out of a zipper on her thigh. Apparently it was a slow day for the school rebels. The place was practically deserted. Of course, Robbie Canetti was there because Robbie Canetti was always there.

He looked up from his notebook when Ed and Gaia entered. "Hi," he said.

Ed said hi. Gaia didn't bother. Ms. Strahan glanced at them, then went back to correcting papers.

Ed wheeled himself to the back corner of the room, and Gaia flung herself into a chair, letting it scrape against the floor loudly. Her leg immediately started to bounce up and down. There was no way she was staying trapped in this box for the next hour.

She leaned forward, pressing her elbows into her knees to stop her legs from spasming. "I have two things to say," she said, looking Ed in the eye. "One, I didn't want to do what I did out there. I really am sorry."

"I know," Ed answered seriously. "What's the second thing?"

"The second thing is that I'm outta here." She stood up and started past him, but Ed grabbed her wrist.

"I know where Sam is," he said.

Gaia froze. Relief, confusion, and disbelief rushed through her, clouding her vision. She fell back into her chair. "What?"

Ed shot his eyes toward Ms. Strahan, then Robbie. When he was sure neither was listening, he whispered, "I know where they're holding him."

It was all Gaia could do to keep from screaming. She wasn't sure if she should hug him or kill him. "Why didn't you tell me this before?"

Ed actually blushed. "You didn't exactly give me a chance back there, G."

"Where is he?" Gaia demanded, feeling a strong urge to hold him upside down and shake the words right out of him.

Clearing his throat, Ed pushed his hands against his armrests and shifted in his chair. The gesture took forever. "He's in Tribeca. I actually pinpointed the street." Ed's expression was all self-satisfaction. Gaia was leaning away from hug and toward kill, but she kept her cool.

"How did you figure it out?" she asked in a whisper.

Ed leaned forward. "I just kept replaying the e-mail," he said excitedly. "By, like, the nine billionth time, I started to register this sound in the background. Over and over, this sound. And I recognized it. It's skateboarders."

"Skateboarders?" Gaia hissed, her shoulders so

tense they were practically touching her ears. "Ed, skateboarders can be anywhere."

"No." Ed shook his head. "This noise was distinct. It was boards on a ramp—an extreme ramp, with a major slope. And I know for a fact there's only one ramp like that in this whole city. I practically used to live there."

His eyes were glassy, and she could tell he really missed this home away from home.

Gaia would have loved to let him slip into a fit of nostalgia, but this wasn't the place, and it definitely wasn't the time.

"Ed."

He rubbed his hand over his face. "Anyway, I heard that sound in the background, and I realized that Sam's got to be somewhere in the vicinity of that ramp. He's gotta be in one of those buildings."

Gaia stood up. "So let's go."

"Go? Gaia, we can't go."

"Ms. Moore?" Ms. Strahan warned. Gaia didn't care.

"Why not?" she asked Ed. "Because we've got detention?" She looked around the room, holding her palms out like a balance, pretending to weigh the options. "Let's see. Sam's life, detention. Detention, Sam's life." She frowned at him. "I'm going."

She started for the door, but Ed reached out and grabbed her wrist.

"Ms. Moore," came another warning.

Ed actually yanked on her arm, tugging her backward and forcing her into her seat. She looked at him for a moment, stunned.

"No, Gaia. Not because we have detention," Ed hissed, his eyes flashing. "Think about it. You know the kidnapper's watching every move you make. You're at his mercy. If he figures out you're planning a search-and-rescue operation, he might just kill Sam on the spot."

"Yeah, but . . ."

"I know you want to swoop in there and rescue Sam," Ed said. "But you have to make sure you're thinking straight."

Gaia sighed in exasperation.

"Even if you could get to Sam without having the lunatic kidnapper catch on, how are you going to get him out?" Ed asked. "The guy's a mess, Gaia. He's weak, remember?"

Gaia felt as if her head were being pumped full of molten lava. She pressed the heels of her hands to her temples and squeezed her eyes shut.

"So why'd you even bother to tell me where he was?"

"Because I knew you'd want to know," Ed whispered, shaking his head "Look, Gaia, I'm aware you're not going to let me tell you what to do. I'm just telling you what I think."

She gave the desktop a good slap. Everyone in the room jumped but her.

"Okay, I've had about enough of this, Ms. Moore," Ms. Strahan said in what Gaia assumed was supposed to be a threatening tone.

"You got something against hearing what I think?" Ed whispered with a grin.

"I've got something against being trapped in a classroom when I should be out doing something constructive," Gaia answered, standing again. "And don't ask me what, because I don't know, but I have to get the hell out of here!"

"Gaia—"

"That's it, Ms. Moore."

But Gaia barely registered the warnings. She was already halfway down the hall.

HEATHER DID NOT LEAVE SCHOOL
immediately following first period.

That would have been the cowardly thing to do, and Heather Gannis was nothing if not brave. She proved that every day, didn't she? Swimming with the sharks (as she secretly referred to her

Rent-a-Cop

friends) with only her Almay pressed powder for armor.

So she'd stayed at school and toughed it out. She'd handled all those pitiful looks they threw at her, the feigned sympathy, the understanding hand pats. It was so patronizing. Didn't they know she knew? Didn't they realize she could see through them like a Victoria's Secret peignoir? They loved that she'd been humiliated. They got off on it.

As soon as the final bell sounded, Heather escaped them all.

And now she was on her way to Sam's dorm.

She walked—all right, so it was more like a sub-dued run—toward Washington Square Park, taking the opportunity to think. There hadn't been a clear thought in her head all day. The rigors of maintaining a stiff upper lip, seeming to be grateful, and acting suitably flustered had taken all her energy. She had also been forced to accept hug after hug after hug from all those guys who said they only wanted to comfort her, but really just saw her grief as perhaps their only chance to press their deprived bodies against her legendary one.

Pigs. Idiot pigs. But, she reminded herself for the twelve zillionth time, she'd invited popularity, worked for it, and now had to live with the conse-quences. What was that old saying? Live by the sword, die by the sword. Yep. Same went for popularity.

By the time she reached Fifth Avenue, Heather was convinced she had it all figured out. Sam had secretly filmed them, and then somehow had carelessly allowed the tape to fall into the wrong hands. The hands of Gaia Moore.

Or maybe it hadn't been carelessness on Sam's part. Maybe it had been part of a horrific conspiracy. Maybe—for some reason she could not even begin to imagine—Sam had taped their encounter, then *given* the tape to Gaia to screen in econ.

That would explain why Gaia had shown up that night. That would explain why Sam had run after her. They were working together to ruin Heather's life.

Why? She had no idea. But she was definitely going to find out.

Heather reached Sam's dorm, stomped into the lobby, and was met by the security guard.

Right. She'd forgotten about that little roadblock.

"Can I help you?" he asked.

Heather smiled automatically. The guy was beefy, maybe in his late twenties. She could tell this rent-a-cop position was probably a dream job for him—second only to his lifelong fantasy of changing his name to the Raunchy Raider and becoming the darling of the professional wrestling circuit.

"Hi," she said. "I'm just going up to visit my boyfriend."

He drew himself up tall. He was obviously very important. "I'll need to see your university ID."

Lucky for Heather she could blush on command. "You think I'm in college?"

The guy smiled. "Aren't you?"

Heather shook her head coyly. "I'm only in high school. But he's expecting me. . . ."

"Sorry, sweetheart."

Don't *sweetheart* me, you pumped-up piece of shit. "Please?" She smiled and gave him her best little head tilt. "Look. He gave me a key."

She produced Sam's dorm key from the back pocket of her jeans. Okay, so he hadn't actually given it to her. She'd stolen his spare copy in a fit of immaturity back when they'd first started getting serious. It had made her feel special to have it—her boyfriend's college dorm room key. And her friends had thought she was beyond lucky. Now her petty crime was about to come in handy.

"Look, honey," meat-for-brains said, "I don't care if the guy gave you his key. I don't care if he gave you his tuition money, all right? The bottom line is, you're not getting in here without a valid New York University ID."

Heather ground her teeth. "Can't you call him? He'll come down and get me."

137

The guard's eyes slid over her body like maple syrup on a stack of pancakes. "I'm sure he will." He picked up the phone. "What's his number?"

She gave it to him. He dialed.

"Busy."

"What?"

"The line's busy."

This threw her. Sam's line was never busy. A black hole formed in her stomach. Maybe he had it off the hook.

Maybe he was so desperate to avoid her that he'd instructed this steroid-shooting side of beef who used too much hair gel not to let anyone fitting her description anywhere near the elevator.

Disgusted, Heather turned on her heel and stalked out onto the cold street.

"SO NOW WHAT?"

Gaia shrugged. "I don't know." Ed had followed her out of detention, and now she was following Ed down the handicap ramp. A late afternoon chill crept into the neck of her sweatshirt, causing goose bumps to break out on her skin. "Maybe they're gonna have me

scale the Empire State Building in my underwear."

"I'd like to see that," Ed joked.

"Seriously. There's got to be another test, doesn't there?" Her eyes made a wide sweep of the area. "But what? When?"

Bring it on, she willed silently. Come on! It was like waiting to throw a punch, or waiting to have one thrown at you. Come and get me. Come and get me.

When they reached the sidewalk, Ed angled his chair to allow a food vendor to pass by with his stout, steaming cart.

"Y'know what's weird?" Ed asked. "The last tests came at you like rapid fire, so where the hell are they?"

"Maybe the guy's taking a coffee break," Gaia deadpanned. "Maybe he's a union kidnapper."

Ed's face became tentatively hopeful. "Or maybe you're done."

"Done?"

"Yeah. Maybe they're satisfied," Ed said with a shrug. "Maybe the next message is gonna be, 'You may reclaim your diabetic boyfriend at your earliest convenience.'"

"Don't call him my boyfriend," Gaia said.

"Yes, ma'am."

Absently Gaia watched the hot dog vendor drag his moving eatery to a halt. When he banged open a metal compartment, the uniquely New York aroma of frankfurters and sauerkraut reached her. Her stomach growled fiercely, and she realized she hadn't eaten a thing since the three bites of bagel she'd had at breakfast.

"Hungry?" she asked Ed.

"Sure."

Gaia approached the vendor. "Two. With the works."

"The works," the guy mumbled, grabbing two empty rolls and placing the hot dogs into them.

Gaia watched as he clumsily spooned relish and onions onto them. More of the condiments wound up in his hand than on the dogs. Well, maybe if the jerk took off those dark glasses and pulled his hat up from over his eyes, he'd be able to see what he was doing and—

"Sam says hi."

Gaia's eyes snapped up to the vendor's face.

He thrust the hot dogs into her hand. Her first instinct was to shove them both up his nose. The guy pulled off his sunglasses and gave her the hands-down wickedest stare she'd ever seen. Anyone else would have passed out from the ferocity of it, but Gaia met his gaze. And, since she *had* been born with whichever chemical component created hunger, took a sloppy bite of the hot dog.

The sham vendor was obviously thrown by her calm.

"Sam says hi," he repeated, less icily. He reached into his apron, removed a piece of paper, and held it out to her.

140

She glanced over her shoulder at Ed. "He's out of hot pretzels," she said sarcastically. "Will you settle for a ransom note?"

Ed was wide-eyed. "God. Are they everywhere?"

Gaia took the note, and seconds later the phony hot dog guy was gone.

She handed Ed his hot dog, which he just sort of stared at, as if he'd never seen one before. Gaia decided to read to herself and give Ed a couple of seconds to recover.

Clearly you did not understand what I meant by HUMILIATION, as you and your friend in the wheelchair are still on speaking terms. Momentary embarrassment in the school corridor was not what I had in mind, Gaia. I wanted him out of your life, but I see this has not happened. For this reason, you will perform another test, the most difficult thus far. Before I return Sam to you this evening, you will be required to . . .

Gaia looked up from the note and blinked at Ed. "What? What does it say?"

"Uh . . . it says I'm doing really well. Listen." She skipped to the final paragraph, cleared her throat, and read aloud. "'Sam will be turned over to you this evening at 10 P.M. in Washington Square Park. Choose

141

any pathway. I will find you. FYI—Mr. Moon's health is failing, so I suggest you be prompt.'"

"Is that all it says?"

She swallowed hard and nodded. No reason to tell him how personal the kidnapper was getting with his notes. No reason to tell him—

"Man. He must be pretty sick." Ed was looking pale.

"It says I have to get his insulin from his dorm room," Gaia murmured. His room. Like she wanted to revisit that memory anytime in the next century.

Ed nodded. "Hope we can get into his room."

"You'd be surprised how easy it can be," said Gaia, frowning.

"That's if it's unlocked," Ed reminded her.

"True." Her eyes dropped unwillingly to the note, that one sentence . . .

Ed lowered an eyebrow at her. "You okay?"

Gaia nodded.

"Well, you might not be after I make this next suggestion." He took a deep breath. "I think we're going to need Heather."

"Need Heather? For *what?*" Gaia asked. "Fashion advice on what to wear to a hostage rescue?"

Ed tossed his untouched hot dog into a nearby trash container. "For the key to Sam's room. I'm guessing she's the only person we know who might have one."

Gaia felt her muscles tighten with anger. He was

probably right. And the last thing she needed was to get nabbed for breaking and entering. She wouldn't be helping anyone from jail. Having Sam's room key was crucial.

She ate the rest of her hot dog in two angry bites, then glared at him. "Heather it is," she said with her mouth full.

Ed watched her swallow with a look of near disgust. He'd never looked at her like that. But then, she figured she was doing a pretty good impression of a boa constrictor.

"Are you sure you're all right?"

"I'm fine," she lied, glancing at the note again—at another part she hadn't read out loud. At the part that said, "*Kill CJ*."

Loki hovered
there
another
moment,
allowing his
icy laughter
to rain down
on Sam.

a little buzz

"HI."

CJ turned. The woman was talking to him. The beautiful woman in the tight blouse.

He did his little shoulder thing—loosened himself up. Slouched. "Wus'up?"

She smiled. "I've seen you around, you know."

"Yeah? Well, I ain't seen you." At least not in a while. She used to walk through the park every day, but not lately. It was hard to forget a body like that. She smelled great. Expensive. And her legs went on till Tuesday.

"What's your name?"

"CJ."

"Nice to meet you, CJ."

She reached for his hand and shook it. Talk about silky skin.

"Listen, CJ, I don't usually do this sort of thing, but I was hoping you might like to go out with me. Tonight." The way she fixed her eyes on him made things inside his body stir. Things he didn't even know were there.

Brain cramp! This gorgeous, uptown piece of ass was asking him out? Sure as hell sounded like it. For a moment there was no Gaia.

"Uh . . . uh . . ." Damn, he had to get it together.

"Well?"

Shit, this one was friendly. She was pressing her palms against his chest now.

"You don't have plans, do you?" she asked in a husky voice.

Well, as a matter of fact, he did. He was going to kill Gaia tonight. But then again, maybe he could do both.

The woman was giving him this very seductive little pout. "Please say you'll meet me tonight. There's a band playing in the park. And I love to dance. . . ." She pushed her hips against his and swayed. "Do you like to dance?"

CJ nodded. He liked her perfume. It was giving him a little buzz. Smelled like burning flowers or something.

"Good. So it's a date, then?" She tossed her hair back and looked up at him through her thick lashes. "We'll meet tonight, in the park."

"Yeah. Yeah." He backed up from her slightly, trying to play off the fact that every inch of his body wanted to pounce on her right now. No use letting the lady know she had the power. "That'd be cool. In the park."

"I'll meet you at the fountain," she said, making even the word *fountain* sound dirty. "Say . . . nine-thirty?"

"Yeah. sounds good."

"Till then . . ."

"Yeah."

She turned to walk away, and he remembered that walk. He and Marco used to study it. When she'd gone half a block, he called out to her. "Yo, girl. What's your name?"

147

She didn't bother to answer.

TO: L
FROM: E
RE: CJ

Arrived in NYC early and met with pawn. He'll
meet me in the park at nine-thirty.

If all goes as well as this, he should be dead
before the band plays its first set.

LOKI CRUMPLED THE FAXED MEMO AND

dropped it into the wastebasket.

"Dead before the first set?"
He smiled sardonically. "That's
what I like to hear." His laughter
was an ugly, guttural rumble in
his throat. He turned to Sam.

Poor, poor Sam.

Dying, really, right before
his eyes. A shame.

What the Kidnapper Said

Loki walked toward his
hostage, who was huddled in a shivering heap on the
floor, and studied him in silence for a long moment.

Well, he could understand what his niece saw in

148

the boy. He was certainly nice-looking. At least, he had been, before that unfortunate incident in which his face collided with that fist. Tsk, tsk. And, of course, his medical condition was really `taking its toll.`

"Sam?" Again, louder. "Sam!"

The boy lifted his head slightly and let out a ragged breath.

"Sam Moon," said Loki thoughtfully, rolling the name over his taste buds as though it were a new wine he was tasting. "Tell me about yourself, Sam."

The only reply was `the shuddering of Sam's body.`

"Cat got your tongue, boy?" Loki sneered. "Ah, yes. Just as well. I generally prefer to do the talking in situations such as these. I do so enjoy being in control."

He was circling Sam now, like `the predator he was.` "You're aware, I imagine, that my niece is quite taken with you?" His eyes turned hard as he stared at the prone form before him.

Loki stopped walking, folded his arms across his chest, and glared down at Sam. "That, as you must understand, is not an easy thing for an uncle to accept. I wonder, would you be worthy of her? Because an uncle has certain expectations for his only niece, Sam. He wants the best for her, wants only her happiness. I know it may not seem that way, given current circumstances, but it is true. Gaia, you might say, `has become my whole world.`"

Loki lifted his foot and used the toe of one of his three-hundred-dollar wing tips to give Sam's languid body a hard nudge. "So tell me, Sam Moon," he demanded. "Are you the boy who will make Gaia's dreams come true?"

Loki hovered there another moment, allowing his icy laughter to rain down on Sam.

Then in a voice so slick and close to silence that Loki barely heard it himself, he asked Sam Moon `one last question.`

After that he walked away, the heels of his expensive shoes drumming the highly polished floor of the loft.

He didn't turn around.

He should have.

HE FELT THE LAUGHTER BEFORE HE

heard it. An ugly rumble from across the room. Guttural, like an animal choking.

What the Hostage Heard

The first footsteps—approaching. A presence, near. Then, words:

`Sam Moon.`

`I enjoy . . . control.`

Gaia . . . taken with you . . . my whole
world.

A kick to his rib cage. A shouted question:

. . . dreams come true?

And then, in the slightest whisper:

Do you love her, Sam?

Sam's bruised eye throbbed as he lifted his head.
He had not attempted to use his voice in nineteen
hours, but with what he sincerely believed might be
the very last breath in his body, over the sound of fad-
ing footsteps, Sam answered.

"Yes."

Gaia and Heather.

When you look at them and take them at face value, one might wonder how one person (namely, me . . . and possibly Sam) could love them both in one lifetime.

Gaia is tall, blond, powerful, and favors brown clothing.

Heather is shortish, brunette, a slave to the masses, and never wears brown unless a respected fashion writer tells her it's the "new black."

But Gaia and Heather are more alike than the general public might think.

The first similarity? They'd both kill me if they heard me say that.

The list goes on.

Neither one of them is as brave as she thinks she is. They both have a lot of secrets. (Heather's I pretty much know, Gaia's I'm not sure I want to know.) They both have trust issues. I've never known two people with such a gift for sarcasm. They are both extremely beautiful.

And they both have a thing for college guys.

So it's not hard to see why one guy could love them both in the same lifetime.

The real question is, why do I bother?

"Heather? It's Jeff Landon. . . . So, uh, are you busy Saturday night?"

phone tag

RRRING. CLICK. BEEP.

"You've reached the Gannis residence. Please leave a message at the beep. Thank you."

"Heather! It's Megan. Oh my God! I am still so totally freaked out by what happened at school today! I can*not* believe Sam, like, actually taped you guys doing it. And gave it to *Gaia*? That's like— ugh—*so* unbelievably tasteless. It's like, okay, why don't we all just go on *Jerry Springer*? I mean, like, what if you were wearing weird underwear or something, y'know? Okay, so, like, call me as soon as you get in. Bye."

Click. Beep.

What kind of idiot was Megan? She knew Heather didn't have her own phone line. She knew Heather's answering machine was in the family room, where anyone could overhear a message coming in. Heather's parents were actually really good about not snooping, and they would never purposely listen to an incoming call. But what if they happened to be passing through the family room while Megan was ranting about she and Sam "doing it"? Idiot.

Rrring. Click. Beep.

"Hi, it's Ashley. I skipped school today to get my hair highlighted, but I just heard the best dirt! This

156

morning somebody actually showed a video of people having, like, *sex*—in school! Well, no, I mean, they weren't having sex in school, they showed the video in school. The sex was, like, someplace else. I don't know who was on the tape, though, 'cuz I heard it from Jen, who heard it from Mallory, who heard it from . . . I dunno, like, somebody. But now I'm, like, so bummed that I dropped AP econ! Oh! Hey! You're still in that class, aren't you? So *you* must have seen it. Cool. All right, so call me with the info!"

Click. Beep.

It had been going on all day. She'd already erased at least twenty messages on this very topic. But she refused to take the phone off the hook, in case Sam tried to call.

To explain himself.

To apologize.

To tell her he'd had nothing to do with that damn video.

She'd come home from the disaster at the dorm and spent the last hour lying on the family room sofa, screening calls.

Rrring. Click. Beep.

"Heather! It's Jeff Landon. Heard about your film debut. Whoa. Didn't know you were into that kind of thing. So, uh, are you busy Saturday night?"

Beep.

Heather chucked a throw pillow at the answering

machine. It missed by about three feet and bounced off the top of the television. She sighed, then rolled over onto her stomach. Sam's dorm room key bit into her hip. It was still in the front pocket of her pants. She pulled it out and stared at it for a second before flinging it, too, across the room, where it knocked over a framed photo of her and Sam at a Yankees game.

Rrring. Click. Beep.

"Heather, it's Megan again! Are you there? Pick up! I just heard that band Fearless is playing in the park tonight. The drummer's a total hottie! Wanna go? Maybe it'll, you know, cheer you up or whatever. Call me."

That was it! Heather had officially had it. She was taking the phone off the hook, and for all she cared, Sam could go to hell. Let him call. Let him get a busy signal. Let him come over with a dozen long-stemmed roses and apologize in person, like a normal boyfriend!

She was just reaching for the handset when the phone rang again. She jerked her fingers away as though she'd been shocked, then listened.

Click. Beep.

"Hi, Heather. It's Ed. Fargo. Listen, I realize this call must come as a shock, but I have something really serious I need to talk to you about. It's important. It's . . . uh . . . about Sam. He's in trouble. Well, actually, not trouble. More like danger. There's something we have to get out of his room. We're talking life and death here. Sam's life and death. So we were thinking, since you probably have a key to his room, you would bring it to us. Heather, you've got to help us. . . ."

Heather picked up the handset. The machine shut off, routing Ed's voice directly through the phone as she pressed it to her ear.

"Heather? Are you there?"

She had two words for him: "Who's us?"

The Key

"WHAT DO YOU MEAN, SHE DOESN'T want me involved?"

"I mean," said Ed, wheeling fast to keep up with Gaia's furious pace, "she's all for helping Sam, but she doesn't want you to be a part of it."

"*Part* of it? Part of *it*?" Gaia punched her right fist repeatedly against her thigh as she walked. "Doesn't the airhead realize that I *am* it? Didn't you explain that to her?" Gaia slammed directly into a man in a business suit, sending him sprawling. "Sorry," she mumbled over her shoulder. The guy swore after her but was too busy restuffing his briefcase to give chase.

"No, I didn't. I'm guessing it would have done more harm than good." Ed stopped at the corner, waiting for the light. He glanced warily over his shoulder. Gaia half hoped the suit would come yell at her. She needed a good excuse to hit something.

When Ed had explained that Gaia was involved, the news had, naturally, sent Her Royal Heatherness into convulsions. After some careful negotiations, Ed had managed to get her to agree to discuss it in person—without Gaia.

"So she's not expecting me?" Gaia asked, holding her hair back from her face to keep it from whipping into her eyes.

"No," Ed answered, staring at the rushing traffic.

"Great."

Gaia stopped fuming long enough to check out the neighborhood. It was a little to the east of the area that was really upscale. It wasn't bad. But there was nothing much to recommend it, either. The streets were lined with smallish apartment buildings that were falling into disrepair—chipping paint, cracked moldings, windows scratched with graffiti. Plus it seemed like the garbage hadn't been hauled off in weeks.

"Where are we going?" Gaia asked.

"Heather's."

Gaia lifted an eyebrow in the direction of the

nearest worse-for-wear apartment building. "You mean she doesn't live in some yuppie co-op somewhere in the eighties?"

"Not anymore," Ed said flatly.

They continued in silence for two blocks, then turned a corner and found Heather waiting for them on the sidewalk in front of a nondescript, graying apartment building.

Ed waved.

Heather fired Gaia a hateful look from thirty paces off.

"I told you not to bring her," Heather said, crossing her arms over the front of her suede jacket.

"This is important," Ed told her. "Gaia's involved, whether you like it or not."

Heather looked like a rabid alley cat. She ignored Ed, focusing all her attention on glaring at Gaia. "Are you sleeping with Sam?"

Gaia rolled her eyes. "Oh, give me a break—"

"Are you?" Heather's mouth contorted with fury.

"Heather!" Ed blurted. He wheeled his chair between the two girls. "This isn't about you," he said firmly, leveling her with a stare. "This is about Sam."

Heather glanced at him, a flicker of interest in her eyes. "Right, so what's going on? How do you even know him?"

Gaia let out an exasperated sigh. The girl had a talent for pointless questions.

"It doesn't matter how I know him," Ed said. "What matters is he's been kidnapped."

"Kidnapped?"

The color drained from Heather's face, and Gaia felt her stomach flop.

That was what fear looked like. Gaia found herself fighting back a wave of what could only be called jealousy. She cared for Sam more than anyone would ever know. Yet again she felt deep discomfort at the knowledge that when his life was threatened, she couldn't feel this most basic emotion. But a conscience-free zone like Heather Gannis could. Heather could have natural feelings when the guy they both loved was in danger.

Gaia felt like a voyeur as she watched the tears forming in Heather's eyes. She made herself look away.

"By who? Why?" Heather asked.

"We're not sure," Ed said. "Somebody's holding him hostage."

"Oh my God!"

"We think we can rescue him, but we're running out of time."

"Rescue him? When?"

Probably needs to check her Week-at-a-Glance, Gaia thought cynically. *"Sure, I can pencil in Sam's rescue for tonight—unless there's a sale at Abercrombie."*

"Tonight," said Ed.

Morbidly curious, Gaia watched Heather closely, feeling an inexplicable loneliness. Heather's eyes were so huge, so filled with terror, they threatened to overtake her whole face. She was actually quaking. Gaia couldn't pull her eyes away. She knew what fear looked like. But what did it *feel* like? *What?* And would she ever know the extent of what she was missing?

"Oh my God," Heather said, her voice quivering. "Oh my God, oh my God!"

"Calm down," said Gaia. "Freaking out isn't going to help anything."

"Shut up!" Heather glared at her. "Just shut up and go away."

"She's not going anywhere," said Ed.

"I don't even want to look at her!" Heather sputtered.

"Then don't," snapped Gaia. "Just give us the key so we can—"

"You're not going without me!" Heather exploded. "Sam is still *my* boyfriend. And besides, it's not the key that's the problem. It's the pit bull of a security guard."

Gaia remembered the guard. She'd slipped by him without much trouble on her own, but all three of them? A towhead, a homecoming queen, and a Boy Scout on wheels. They weren't exactly an inconspicuous bunch.

Heather turned to Ed, and her voice ironed itself into a reasonable tone. "I have to do *something*. I want to help him."

"You'll be helping him by giving us the key," said Ed. "That way, we can get his insulin and bring it to him tonight when they release him in the park—"

Gaia brought her hand down hard on Ed's shoulder, effectively shutting him up, but not soon enough. She watched Heather's face as the information was sent to her mental mainframe.

Damn.

"I'm coming with you. I have to be the one to bring it to him." Suddenly she was overcome with either real emotion or really good acting technique. Her eyes filled with tears again, and her breathing was fast and shallow. "He'll need me," she cried. "He'll need me to take care of him. I'm going with you."

"Oh, no!" Gaia exploded. "No way."

"Heather," Ed said calmly, "it's too dangerous."

She glared in Gaia's direction. "Why is it too dangerous for me and not her?"

Gaia wouldn't have minded showing her. Instead she said, "It's dangerous for everyone. Especially Sam. But I'm going because the kidnapper contacted me in the first place."

Something shifted in Heather's eyes as she digested

this information. She seemed to suddenly grow smaller. "Why you?"

"I don't know," Gaia said honestly.

Heather crossed her arms over her chest. "Who do you think you—"

"Yo! Enough." They both snapped their heads around to face Ed. "This isn't helping Sam."

Gaia swore under her breath. Sam's life was in jeopardy, and here she was arguing with Bad-Attitude Barbie. She had to let Ed work on Heather alone for a minute. She turned and headed back toward a small convenience store she'd noticed near the corner.

If all else failed, she could knock Heather's lights out and just take the key.

But something told her that wasn't going to be necessary. Ed would be able to convince her. Maybe it was the residual tenderness she heard in his voice every time he talked to her or about her. Maybe it was the way Heather changed—almost indiscernibly, but still, *changed*—when Ed looked at her, as though something were happening inside her that she didn't want or expect. It was as if Heather were locked out of her own soul and somehow Ed still had the key.

For the life of her, Gaia could not figure out why that annoyed her so much.

But it did.

GAIA WAS COMING OUT OF THE
store, finishing up her Mars
bar, when Ed appeared.

The Ripple Effect

"I've got good news and
bad news," he said.

"Is the bad news that
you couldn't think of anything more original to say
than that?" Gaia asked through a mouthful of nuts
and chocolate. She crumpled the wrapper and shoved
it into her sweatshirt pocket with the two other
chocolate bars she'd bought. Gaia didn't know much
about diabetes, but she thought Sam might need
them.

"So where is she?" Gaia asked, glancing past Ed.

"She'll meet us here in a few minutes," Ed said, stu-
diously avoiding eye contact. "She went inside to get
the key."

Gaia's body rippled with relief. "She's
going to give it up?"

"More or less," Ed answered, picking at the hole in
his sweater.

"I'm not sure that's possible, Ed," Gaia said impatiently.

"She's coming with us to the dorm," Ed said, push-
ing his shoulders back, trying to look defiant.
"There's no way around it."

Gaia tilted her head back, staring up at the rapidly

darkening sky. "Do you think she's gonna be able to keep her head when she sees Sam in the park, all beaten and bloody, being shoved around by some guy in commando gear who's holding a sawed-off shotgun to his head, and who knows what else?"

Ed looked a little white. "She'll be long gone before we get to the park."

Gaia had to bite her lip to keep herself from commenting on his use of the word *we*. He didn't know it yet, but *he* was going to be long gone, too. There was no way she was going to drag Ed into that little scenario. But perhaps it was best not to mention that just yet.

"What makes you so sure she'll be gone?" Gaia asked, leaning back against the brick wall of the convenience store.

Ed smiled and his eyes filled with mischief. Gaia knew what was coming before he said it.

"Because I have a plan."

He didn't
think he
could handle
the humilia-
tion if his
brainless
first-ever
covert-
action plan
crashed and
burned.

ED WHEELED HIS WAY INTO THE

Mission: Not-So-Impossible

dorm and took a look around. The lobby smelled of beer-dampened carpet and the bottle's worth of CK One with which the guard had obviously drenched himself.

Hmm. Ed would have pegged this one for a Brut by Fabergé type. Go figure.

"Hi."

Behind his desk, the guard averted his eyes and gave him a nod.

Typical. Can't look the cripple in the eye.

Ed aimed for the elevator.

Waiting . . . waiting . . .

Okay, so gimme the ID speech already. He checked his watch. Seven twenty-eight. C'mon, buddy. Ask for the card.

Nothing.

Ed hit the elevator button hard. The Neanderthal glanced in his direction and dredged up an awkward grin.

Damn! Don't tell me the quasi-cop is too soft-hearted to hassle a guy in a wheelchair.

Above the elevator, the number 3 lit up. It would

reach ground level any second, and Ed would be able to roll right on. No distraction, no clear avenue for Gaia and Heather.

Over his head, the number 2 blinked orange.

"Excuse me," he said. "I'm heading up to see a friend, but I'm not sure I'll be able to find his room. Those letters and numbers are kinda confusing. Can ya help me out?"

Not until you see my ID, right? Go ahead, say it!

"The letter stands for the wing," the guard explained. "A is to the right, B to the left. There are four rooms to a suite and they're all clearly marked."

"Thanks," Ed muttered. He was starting to sweat. He didn't think he could handle the humiliation if his first-ever covert-action plan crashed and burned.

For a second the guy just looked at Ed and seemed to be trying to decide what to do.

C'mon, brainless. Card me, already. Then the elevator announced itself with a loud *ding*, and the door opened.

"I've never been in any of these dorms before," Ed said. He raised his voice a few decibels louder than necessary. "I don't go here."

There! Now he's got no choice.

The Neanderthal cleared his throat. "Listen, pal," he said in a regretful tone. "I really can't let you up if you don't have an ID."

Finally! Ed narrowed his eyes as the elevator door slid closed. "What do you mean?"

"University policy. Sorry." The guard shoved his beefy hands into his pockets. Damn, he was uncomfortable. "Nonstudents can't—"

"Nonstudents?" Ed challenged, spinning his chair toward the guard. "You sure you don't mean people in wheelchairs?"

The guy looked at him, waylaid. "Huh?"

"C'mon, man. You know the real reason you're not letting me get on this elevator is because I can't walk into it on my own two feet," Ed said, his face growing red. He should get an Oscar for this one.

"No. That ain't it." Now the Neanderthal was sweating, too. "It's just—"

"Yeah, right! I've seen this crap before," Ed shouted, gripping the armrests on his chair. "It's always the chair. It's discrimination."

Now the guy was getting pissed. "It has nothin' to do with the chair. It's the rule. No ID, no admittance."

Ed gave him a disgusted look, then turned his chair again and reached for the elevator button.

"Hey!" barked the guard, hurrying out from behind the desk. "I told you—"

"What are ya gonna do?" Ed chuckled wickedly. "Hit me?"

With that, they began to argue in earnest.

"ALL RIGHT, WE'RE GOING IN," GAIA

7:31

said from her position outside Sam's dorm.

Heather rolled her eyes, but when Gaia pushed through the lobby door, Heather followed. Ed had managed to lure the guard out from behind his station, so Gaia and Heather tiptoed behind the guard's back and slipped into the stairwell.

All politeness, Gaia held the door open, allowing Heather to go through first. No idiot, Heather shot Gaia a suspicious look, but Gaia could practically see her train of thought. Heather didn't want Gaia behind her, but the thought of getting to Sam's room first was tempting.

Heather sneered at Gaia and brushed past her.

"You're welcome," Gaia snapped in a whisper.

Heather started to jog, and Gaia followed close behind. It was torture having Heather's scrawny ass in her face, but it was going to be worth the sacrifice in about five seconds. Gaia let Heather get up three half flights of stairs before she made her move.

Gaia reached up and grabbed Heather's ankle, sending the girl sprawling on the concrete landing between the first and second floors.

"Get off me!" Heather yelled.

Holding Heather down with one hand, Gaia seized the key from Heather's grasp with a mercury-fast

173

action that would have done even the most seasoned New York purse snatcher proud.

Gaia pulled Heather to her feet. "Sorry, but it was necessary," Gaia muttered.

"I-I'm going to-to *kill* you," Heather shrieked, struggling to no avail.

"Me first," Gaia said, trying not to enjoy the terror in Heather's eyes. She wasn't going to kill her, of course, though it was tempting. She did, however, need to shove Heather down a few steps, both so she could get to Sam's room without further interference, and so the overweight guard could catch Heather.

Gaia gave Heather one hard push, and Heather yelped. She stumbled down the half flight and landed at the bottom with a thud. It looked like it hurt at least a little.

At that moment Gaia heard Ed yelling at the guard. Right on cue.

"Some chick just snuck into the stairs! Yeah! Yes! I swear! Brown hair! Pink shirt!"

Heather was struggling to her feet as Gaia heard the sound of the lobby door to the stairs banging open.

It was time to get out of there.

"Later, Heather!"

Gaia took off up the stairs. She heard Heather start after her, but the guard had already caught up.

"Where do you think you're going?" he asked, panting.

"Get *off* me!" Heather screamed. "Gaia! *Gaia!*"

Gaia smiled as she sprinted down the fourth-floor hallway.

GAIA STOOD OUTSIDE THE DOOR OF

Dorm Room Revisited

room B4 and held her breath. The last time she'd been here Sam had been making love to Heather.

How could she bring herself to go in there?

"Don't be such a sentimental idiot," Gaia told herself, shaking off the self-inflicted melodrama. "This is a college dorm room. I should have a nickel for every sexual encounter that's taken place in here."

She slid the key into the lock.

The doorknob fell off in her hand.

For a moment she just stared at it.

Son of a bitch!

The damn thing had been broken all along! Not even lockable. So they hadn't needed the key after all.

175

And, by association, they hadn't needed Heather. What a waste of time!

Then again, it had provided the opportunity for Gaia to give Heather a good hard shove. Truth be told, that had actually been kind of cathartic.

She opened the door. And there it was. Sam's bed.

Gaia stepped into the room, keeping her mind on her task. Insulin. Must find insulin. Don't even look at that framed photograph of Heather over there on the dresser. Could she possibly be wearing any more lip gloss?

Insulin, damn it! What was the matter with her?

Gaia seemed to remember the stuff had to be re-frigerated. Her eyes swept the room and found a minifridge in the corner. She opened the door. Two bottles of mineral water, a small mountain of those plastic packets of duck sauce that come with Chinese takeout, and a small zippered nylon case.

She opened the case. Pamphlet of instructions. Vials. Syringe.

A wave of emotion washed over her. It was like holding the definition of *vulnerable* in her hands. Sam—perfect, brilliant, gorgeous Sam—had this to contend with. This frailty. This tiny physiological flaw, this infinitesimal defect in body chemistry. This burden. This disadvantage.

Tell me about it.

She stuffed the case into the oversized pocket of her cargo pants, then got up to leave. But there was that damn bed again.

Gaia hesitated perhaps a fraction of a millisecond. Then she threw herself onto the bed. Don't think about the fact that the last time you saw it, Heather was between the sheets. Think about Sam.

Sam's bed.

Sam's sheets. Sam's pillow. Gaia buried her face in it, breathing deeply. Maybe there was something of him still clinging to the pillowcase—an eyelash, maybe, or an echo of a dream.

"Oh, God, Sam . . . I'm so sorry."

She clutched the pillow to her body.

I don't want to kill anybody, her brain said for the hundredth time since she'd read the last directive. *I don't want to kill. I don't want to kill.*

Images flooded her mind, drowning her brain: Sam at the chessboard. Sam coming to see her in the hospital. Sam on the park bench.

And then it was CJ. CJ chasing her down Broome Street. CJ in the police lineup. CJ holding a gun to her head. And firing. And . . .

Gaia sat bolt upright.

She knew what to do.

Rook to knight four.

Queen's knight. Castle. Pawn.

Wrrrzzzzzzzzz. Clank.

I see Gaia's fingers on a chess piece. She pushes the smooth, angular knight with her index finger. And Zolov clicks his false teeth in appreciation of her genius.

The sound bullies me.

Wrrrzzzzzzzzz, clank, wrrzz. I only want to sleep. Sleep. But my levels are off, and my own blood poisons me.

Time is running—check.

Checkmate.

Blackness surrounds me, cold, flat, then it erupts into a pattern of squares. Clean, sharp-cornered red bruises interrupt my blackout. The board spins in its own dimension until I am above it, leaning, knowing, playing. I hear the sound of the plastic piece scraping the cardboard squares.

Wrrrzzzzzzzzz.

The hunger is huge. The blackness quivers. I place my hand around Gaia's on her knight.

And sleep.

Oh, God. Is this what forgiveness feels like?

bring it on

GAIA FOUND ED WAITING AT THE

southwest corner of Fifth Avenue and Tenth Street—the designated meeting spot. It was dark out, and he sat in a square of light pouring out of the lobby of the building behind him.

"Get it?" he asked.

"Got it." She nodded, patting the nylon case inside her pocket. "C'mon, let's go. There's somewhere I have to be."

Gaia started walking toward the park, and Ed quickly caught up with her.

"How'd it work out with Heather and the guard?" Gaia asked, hoping to keep him from asking where exactly she had to be.

A shadow of guilt crossed his face. "It got pretty hairy. She was ballistic when they tossed her out."

"Tossed her out, huh?" asked Gaia, savoring the image. "You mean that literally, right?"

"Pretty much," Ed said. "From what I overheard, it seems our little Heather tried to get in to Sam's room earlier today. The guard recognized her and thought she was some crazed stalker, so he totally ignored her when she was shouting about you getting away. They took her to the main security office. She fought him like you wouldn't even believe, kicking, swearing, snorting...."

"So she didn't get around to implicating you?" Gaia asked, glancing up at the arch at the north end of Washington Square Park. It was illuminated at night, and Gaia couldn't help thinking it was beautiful. It was kind of like a beacon.

"I'm sure she tried," Ed said, following her gaze. "But no way were they gonna believe her." He shook his head. "Man, I feel sorry for the guy who had to interrogate her."

"What time is it?" she asked. If he noticed she wasn't really paying attention to the conversation, he didn't say anything.

He checked his watch. "Only eight ten. We've got plenty of time before we have to go to the park."

"Excuse me?" Gaia said. "*We've* got plenty of time?"

"What is it with you women and pronouns today, huh?" Ed asked.

Gaia shoved her hands into her pockets. Her fingers automatically closed around the candy bars. "I'm serious, Ed. I'm going to do this alone."

Ed scoffed. "No, you're not."

"Yes, I am."

"No, you're not."

"Yes, I . . ." Gaia threw up her hands. "Ed, this isn't open to debate. You said it yourself to Heather—it'll be dangerous."

He had no idea how dangerous, of course, because

ne was unaware of the last note's final directive. But she wasn't about to tell him she'd be murdering a gang member in cold blood this evening, which wasn't exactly the sort of thing that required an escort.

He stopped wheeling. "And you think just because I'm in this chair . . ."

"Oh, please! Save the politically correct guilt trip for somebody who gives a shit, okay?" Gaia spat out. "Yes, you're in a wheelchair. Yes, in this case it's a liability. It makes you slow, and obvious, and a real easy target."

Ed looked at her a moment, then turned away.

Damn. She hadn't meant that the way it sounded. Well, no, actually she'd meant it exactly the way it sounded. It was the truth, for God's sake. Of course, she'd neglected to mention her most important reason for not wanting him there.

"Listen," she said, not quite gently, but as close to it as she could stand to get. "I'm not saying this stuff to hurt your feelings—if I wanted to do that, I'd tell you what I really think of your taste in clothes." He didn't face her, but she could feel him smiling. "I've got to do this myself, Ed. Because . . ."

At last he turned. "Because?"

"Because if anything happened to you . . ." Gaia pulled her jacket close to her as the wind picked up, and sighed. "If anything happened to you, the world would be a much sadder place," she finished so quietly she wasn't certain the breeze had left any of her words for Ed to hear.

A few hundred years went by before Ed finally spoke. "Thanks, Gaia."

"Yeah, whatever." Gaia picked at a hangnail. "Let's not make this a mush fest, okay? You know you're, like, my only friend on the planet. So what good would it do me to let you take a bullet to the skull?"

She handed him Heather's key, careful not to let her hand touch his.

"Get this back to her," she said

"Don't you want to keep it?"

Gaia shook her head. "He gave it to her, not to me."

"Yeah," Ed replied softly, lowering his eyes. "I know exactly what you mean."

She figured he was thinking back on his bygone relationship with Heather, because his tone was tender in the extreme. She sighed again.

"I gotta go," she said, looking off toward the center of the park.

He raised his eyes, surprised. "Now?"

"Yeah, well . . . I have to stop back at my place. I've gotta get something." Something she really didn't want to get. Something that should just have been left in its uninspired hiding place forever.

"What?"

Gaia hesitated, waiting for an appropriate lie to shove its way to the front of her brain. Then her mind oomed back to the Duane Reade bag, the cop, Renny.

"Tampons."

"Oh." Ed's face flushed faster than Gaia had ever thought possible. "Well, uh . . . be careful."

She grinned. "With the tampons?"

"Gaia!"

"I'll be okay." Her brows knitted together, and she stared at Ed seriously. "I'll be okay as long as you stay far, far away from the park tonight."

Ed sighed and shook his head. "Fine."

She was three steps away when she turned around again. "Promise me, Ed. Promise me you will *not* come to the park."

He nodded. "I promise."

If she hadn't been thinking so hard about killing CJ, she might have recognized that Ed was as good a liar as she was.

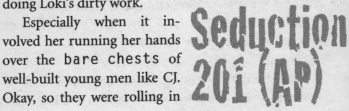

ELLA WOULD NEVER GET TIRED OF doing Loki's dirty work.

Especially when it involved her running her hands over the bare chests of well-built young men like CJ. Okay, so they were rolling in

Seduction 201 (AP)

the dirt behind a bush off some pathway in the park—not exactly a classy setting. But she knew how to make the best of any situation.

This one was as sexy as he was mean. She'd always liked that combination.

Marco was good. CJ was much, much better.

And he was amazed by her. Well, of course. He was probably used to teenage sluts with grungy hair and too much black eyeliner. He'd never seen actual silk this close before, let alone touched it.

Now, here's where I sigh for him, nice and deep—make him think I've never had anything this good before.

CJ smiled hungrily.

He's so proud of himself. Look at him showing off! It was almost cute.

That's right. One more button.

He breathed her name. Or what he thought was her name. So amazed. So grateful. He had no idea there was a blond assassin on her way there to murder him.

Well . . . if you've gotta go, this is definitely the way to spend your final hour.

He asked why she was laughing.

"I always laugh when I'm ready," she said seductively. "Are you ready?"

Over his shoulder, she checked her watch. Ten till ten. Then there was a sound from a nearby tree. It was a miracle she even heard it over CJ's moaning and heavy breathing. It was a signal: She's here.

Okay, you darling, dangerous boy . . . let's make this quick.

"Yes, CJ! Yes . . . *Yes!*" Perfect timing! And then . . .

"CJ, I hear someone. . . ."

He rose to his knees with a nice lazy smile, tugged up his jeans, and peered through the leaves.

"Shit!"

"What is it?" He was looking for his shirt. No luck.

"Shit. It's her. I gotta go. Sorry."

The "sorry" threw her a bit. I suppose I have to act like I care. "Don't go, CJ! Wait!"

He didn't even realize she'd taken his gun.

He leaned down and gave her a hard kiss on her mouth and told her he'd see her again; he *promised*— in this rough, almost heartbreaking voice—that he'd see her again. Then he took off. She sat up, buttoning her blouse, surveying the damage to her skirt.

Gaia, he's all yours.

GAIA ENTERED WASHINGTON SQUARE Park.

It was nine forty.

The concert was supposed to start at ten. The band was already doing sound checks. The squeal of feedback from

Parks and Wreck

the microphones echoed above the gathering crowd. Gaia watched the arriving fans with a combination of interest and longing.

What must it be like, she wondered, to have nothing else to do on a Monday night besides go to a concert in the park? No gangbangers to ice, no hostages to free...

What's it like just to be normal?

Well, she decided, looking around at the crowd, *normal* was a relative term—this was the West Village, after all. Tattoos and navel rings required.

So where the hell was CJ?

It was almost funny that she was looking for him for a change. The problem was, she hadn't expected to actually have to look. He'd been like clockwork in the past, always just sort of there—lurking, looming, stalking. Tonight, though, when it was absolutely imperative that their paths cross, he was a no-show.

How nauseatingly ironic was that?

Reasoning that even a brainless wonder like CJ might find the band concert too public a place to hunt his prey, Gaia plunged into the semidarkness of the pathway that led to Washington Square West.

She'd noticed that morning that a few leaves had begun to change. Change. Die. It was all in how you looked at it, but where just weeks ago there had been nothing but thriving greenery, there were now little glimpses of color. Throughout the expanse of billowing green, the brown-red leaves clung like scabs. They drew the eye automatically, as though to remind you that death refused to go unnoticed.

The shadows engulfed her, and the trees muffled the sound of the band and the band watchers. It was odd—even after all the horrific stuff that had happened to her in this park, she still liked it, liked the way it smelled, liked the way it rustled. She marveled at the weird, restless peacefulness of the place.

Even tonight. Even with a .38 in her waistband and CJ on the prowl.

And Sam . . .

Was he here somewhere? What if the kidnapper wasn't really going to release him? What if . . .

No. She couldn't dwell on that possibility. Sam was here. He had to be.

Did the kidnapper have him in a half nelson behind some tree, a rag stuffed in his mouth to keep him quiet? Then again, if Sam was in as bad shape as the last note had indicated, none of that would be necessary, would it?

So maybe he was writhing in the dirt in unbearable agony, clinging to his gorgeous existence by a mere thread, closer—like the drying leaves—to death than to life.

Gaia's skin prickled; her heart was practically doing the lambada in her chest. She wouldn't have

Sam back until she dealt with CJ. So where was he?

"C'mon, you dirtbag. Show your ugly face."

Even as she whispered it, she heard him. He was maybe fifteen feet behind her but approaching fast. And then he was on her, his hand slamming down on her shoulder, jerking her around to face him.

She reached out with both hands, grabbed him around the neck, and yanked his face down to connect with her head.

Nose—busted. No question. Good. It would go nicely with the sling on his arm. He staggered backward, groaning. "You bitch!"

"Whatever." Gaia nailed him with a series of front kicks to his gut, then spun around, swinging her left leg in a high arc that landed like a wrecking ball against the side of his jaw.

He fell sideways, hitting the pavement with a rib-bashing thud. Gaia pressed her foot between his shoulder blades, pinning him to the ground while she reached into the waist of her pants for the gun.

"You know," she said through clenched teeth, pressing the gun into the flesh behind his right ear, "as much as you really do deserve to die a very painful death . . ."

He flinched as the sole of her sneaker dug deeper into his back.

"As much as you deserve it . . ."

She sighed and lifted her foot. It took him a second to recognize he was free. As soon as he did, he leaped to his feet, and Gaia found herself making the very incongruous observation that this idiot was running around the park at night in October without a shirt on.

He stood very still, staring at her. She held the gun about an inch from his chest.

She had to make it look real without actually killing him. Had to make it look as though she'd tried and failed.

She cocked the hammer. "Hit me," she said, slicing her voice down to a whisper.

"Huh?" He was looking at her as though she were nuts. Maybe she was.

"Hit me," she snarled again, waving the gun.

CJ, obviously, was not very good at following directions.

She leaned closer to him. And wanted to gag. *Smoked rose petals.* Another divergent thought: The freaky witch in Soho is scamming Ella good. Unless . . .

Gaia ducked. CJ's heavy fist caught her in the cheekbone, throwing her slightly off balance. Good enough. She aimed the gun into a tree and fired.

Apparently CJ was only just realizing he'd left his own firearm elsewhere. He froze.

Gaia stumbled a little for dramatic effect, then pointed the gun at him. "Look out, asshole. This one's gonna be closer."

She aimed and fired. The bullet passed so close to CJ's face he could have kissed it.

"That's two," she whispered, watching as CJ fell to his knees and covered his head with his arms. He was begging her not to shoot.

`Again she pulled the trigger.`

CJ winced.

And Gaia whispered, "Bang!"

She had to. Because the bullet that should have been loaded in the third chamber of the gun's barrel was safely hidden in a Duane Reade bag under Gaia's bed.

It was as if eternity made itself visible, swelling around her, slowing the spin of the earth. Gaia swore she saw leaves changing in the chasm of time that elapsed between the steely click of the trigger and CJ's moment of recognition.

`No bullet.`

She gave him a wicked smile. "Déjà vu, huh?"

That's when he ran.

Gaia let out a huge rush of breath, then swung her gaze across the shadows that shrouded the path. She knew the kidnapper was out there somewhere, watching. "Hope you fellas got all that," she muttered. "Hope you bought it."

Her answer was two heavy hands coming down on her shoulders. `Hard.`

Evidently they hadn't bought it at all.

She could
fight like a
machine,
full force,
pumped on
fury and
desire.

eyes

like

hers

OKAY, SO MAYBE LYING RIGHT TO her face wasn't exactly the best way to make her fall in love with him. But what choice did he have?

911

"Promise me you will *not* come to the park tonight."

Yeah. Right.

Sure, she was gutsy. Sure, she was powerful, and capable, and—all right, he'd even give her deadly. But she was his. At least in his heart she was his, and even a—what was it she'd called him? A liability? Yeah. Even a liability like him knew that you absolutely, positively did not let the love of your life do something like this alone.

So he followed her.

The band crowd was a good cover. He had to keep his distance on the path, though.

She still hadn't spotted him. He was at least twenty yards behind and to her left, in the shadow of a rest room building. He didn't have a weapon; he didn't even have the use of his legs. He did, however, have a cell phone, which he would use to dial 911 the minute it looked like Gaia was in trouble.

What was he thinking? It always looked like Gaia was in trouble. What he meant was, the minute it looked like Gaia was out of her league. That's when he'd call for help.

Ed watched as a figure emerged from the bushes, and when he recognized it, he felt fear more intense than he could ever have imagined. It was that gang punk CJ. The one who'd tried to kill her.

"Shit!" Keeping his eyes glued to Gaia, he flipped the phone open. *(Power . . . 9 . . . 1 . . .)* "Whoa! Nice head butt!" *(End)* Man, could she kick! Bam, bam, bam!

She had the looks of a supermodel and the speed of Jean Claude Van Damme. Ooh! Right in the jaw. Nice. CJ went down.

Another cramp of fear gripped Ed when he saw Gaia reach into the waistband of her pants. What the hell was she doing with a gun? And what the hell was she standing there *talking* to CJ for?

Ed's heart jerked in his chest, and then he was watching CJ hit her! The bastard!

(9 . . . 1 . . .)

Holy shit! She fired, missed, but ha! The sound had sent CJ to his knees. Okay, she was back in control. *(End)*

The next shot was close! And then she was pulling the trigger again. And . . .

No bullet?

(9 . . . 1 . . . 1 . . . Send)

"Ed?"

He looked up. "Heather?"

GAIA'S ARMS WERE PINNED BEHIND

her back when the man appeared from out of the bushes. He was dressed—appropriately enough, Gaia supposed—in black. Black slacks, very expensive black sweater, and black shoes, also pricey. She immediately discarded any assumptions that the kidnapper was somehow connected with CJ's scrubby little street gang. These guys were big-time crime. Money. Maybe even brains.

Men in Black

"You failed!" growled Mr. Monochromatic.

Gaia shrugged as best she could with the compromised use of her arms. "I tried."

"Not good enough!"

"It's not my fault you boneheads loaded the gun wrong!" Gaia reasoned.

"Shut up!"

She rolled her eyes. "Fine, I will."

Gaia struck like lightning. She shoved her elbow upward, a nice crack to the underside of her captor's chin, freeing her arms. Before the man in black even had time to advance, she'd delivered one powerful jab to the back of guy number one's neck, knocking him out. He hit the ground like a rag doll.

Then, in one graceful sweep, Gaia turned and wrapped the man in black up in a headlock, pressing

196

the gun—the fourth chamber of which did contain a bullet—to his temple. "I'd prefer to let this do my talking for me, anyway."

The guy grunted.

"I want Sam!" she called to the darkness. "Now. Or this guy's dry cleaner is gonna be looking for a way to get brains out of cashmere!"

Somehow, impossibly, this little corner of the park seemed to be deserted. Had they cleared the area or something?

The guy laughed.

Gaia made herself ignore it. "A trade!" she shouted. "Sam for this guy. Right now. Or I blow his freakin' head off."

The guy laughed again. Gaia arched an eyebrow. He wasn't supposed to be laughing. He should have been begging his buddies to make the trade, save his life.

"What's so funny?" she demanded.

"Shoot me," the guy said. "He won't care."

"What's that supposed to mean?" Gaia asked. "Who won't care?"

"I mean," gurgled the man in black (because Gaia's forearm was still crushing his esophagus), "my employer won't give a damn." The mirth had vanished from his voice now. "He'll probably kill me himself for this."

Damn it! Gaia loosened her grip but didn't release him. She had to think. She had to . . .

Sam!

He was there. Being pushed out from behind a stand of broad oaks by another black-clad villain.

Gaia's heart lurched. Oh, God, Sam! He looked half dead. Gaia had never seen skin so pale before in her life. His face was covered with a sheen of sweat that matted his dirty, greasy brown hair to his forehead. One of his eyes was swollen shut, and the other twitched like a dying bee's wing. There was a spot of blood beneath his right nostril. The jerk in the suit was dragging him like a sack of flour.

Gaia was so overwhelmed with grief that she almost let go of her own charge. She caught herself in time, though, gave him a nice whack with the butt of the gun, then let him crumple to the ground, unconscious.

"Sam!" she screamed.

Did he flinch? Had he heard? Hard to tell. She made a move to go to him, but his captor had suddenly produced an automatic weapon.

And he was aiming it directly at her heart.

"JESUS!" IF ED WEREN'T ALREADY sitting down, he might have passed out. "Heather!"

She was standing there, holding **Hysteria**

the cell phone she'd just snatched out of his hand. He could hear the operator's voice coming through the mouthpiece.

"Hello? Nine-one-one emergency? Hello?"

Apparently Heather was oblivious. She punched the end button.

"How dare you feed me to the wolves like that!" Heather fumed, hands on hips.

He quite seriously wished he could strangle her. "Heather, listen. I'm not kidding around. You have got to get out of here!"

"You can't tell me what to do, Ed," she spat out, her eyes wild. "It's not like we're going out anymore."

Like he'd ever told her what to do when they were together. He decided to chalk that inane remark up to hysteria, which she was clearly on the verge of.

"Heather . . ."

"Where the hell is that little bitch?" she demanded. "And where is Sam? He'd better be all right, or I swear I'm holding you and Gaia responsible. Now, where are they?"

Ed clenched his teeth and jabbed his finger in the direction of a spot on the pathway, roughly twenty yards ahead. "There they are."

Heather looked.

Fortunately, he was able to reach up and flatten his hand over her mouth in time, or her shriek would have certainly given them away.

HE SLAMMED THE SILENCER ONTO

his .44, then stepped out onto the path in front of CJ, who skidded to a flailing halt. The kid had his gun now. He must have found it and grabbed it so that he could go back and finish Gaia off.

Father/Hood

That wasn't going to happen.

Blood still gushed from his nose, and his bare chest was scraped raw. When he saw the gun, his dark eyes got huge. He lifted his hand and aimed at the gunman's chest. That was all that was needed.

Perhaps the last thought ever to register in CJ's brain was something along the lines of He's got eyes like her.

The bullet hit him just above the bridge of his ruined nose, right in the place where all thoughts began.

And ended.

He remained on his feet a good five seconds, a tiny rivulet of crimson trickling from the corner of his mouth, his eyes bulging with what looked more like surprise than anything else.

Then his knees buckled.

And he began to fall.

And with the soundless echo of the boy's last, unspoken plea raging in his mind, Tom Moore disappeared into the darkness before CJ even hit the ground.

GAIA HEARD IT, LIKE SOMETHING OUT

Boogie Knights

of a dream.

A song. What was it? She knew it. Her father used to like it. An oldie. The lead singer's intro over the sound system came floating through the cool night to reach Gaia.

"A classic from the seventies . . . 'Rescue Me,' by Aretha Franklin . . . so let's boogie!"

Boogie? Oh, please.

And then the bouncy tune, and in the singer's gravelly West Village voice, the lyrics: "Rescue me, I want your tender charms, 'cause I'm lonely . . ."

Great. So now the hostage rescue had a sound track.

A surge of memory nearly blinded Gaia as the familiar song wrapped itself around her. Her mother and father, one night in the cozy family room of their house. The radio blaring. It was a classic even then. "Rescue Me." She was six. Laughing. So were they. Dancing. All of them. They were dancing.

Rescue me. Rescue me.

The scream ripped itself from her throat, drowning out the distant melody. Gaia threw herself at the man with the gun, slapping his arm out of the way, sending the gun spiraling into the night sky. He lunged for her, and Sam, unsupported, slipped to the ground.

Her fist plowed into the guy's abdomen, lifting him off his feet. Her foot slammed into his rib cage. She heard him grunt. "Ugh!"

Ugh. We have an ugh. Do I hear an ummphff? She grabbed a handful of his hair and shoved his face down hard against her knee.

"Ummphff!"

We have an ummphff, ladies and gentlemen!

The guy dropped forward, landing on his hands.

Gaia closed by giving him a good old-fashioned kick in the ass. His chin hit the pavement with a sound like breaking glass.

And then her own breaking began—the breaking down, the shutting off, the surrender of all strength. She was familiar with the experience; it happened every time. She could fight like a machine, full force, pumped on fury and desire. Her might was boundless, but only as long as that fuel was in supply. This fight had sucked up every ounce of energy she possessed.

And now she was spent. Her knees softened. Her limbs tingled. Breathing took on an entirely new caliber of effort.

And the lead singer of the band sang, "Rescue me."

It wasn't just in her head, as it seemed. It was blasting through most of the park. She staggered toward Sam, fumbling in her pocket for his insulin, and went down on her knees beside him.

"Hang on," she whispered. At least she thought she whispered it. Maybe she just thought it. He opened his good eye—just a slit, but still, it opened. "Hang on."

She prepared the syringe according to the directions she'd forced herself to memorize on her way from her house to the park. In her weakened state, the needle seemed to weigh a thousand pounds, and then it was entering Sam's flesh. Swift, smooth. Strangely intimate. She was injecting life back into him.

She withdrew the needle. The night spun in slow circles. The singer sang, "Rescue me." Gaia told herself to get up. Stand. Run. For help. But she couldn't seem to lift herself from the pavement.

As it turned out, she didn't have to. The guy in the black sweater was on his feet again. He grabbed Gaia and hauled her up. Her legs buckled. He was crushing her against him, her back to his chest.

Oh. A knife. At her throat. How inconvenient.

And Sam. On the ground, stirring now.

The shot came from behind her. An excellent shot, piercing her captor's shoulder but leaving her untouched. He went down, screaming.

She staggered forward a few steps and landed in the grass.

A man—a golden-haired man—thundered onto the scene. A police officer? No. The Incredible Hulk?

A knight. Yes. A valiant knight.

To rescue me.

Gaia wanted to smile but couldn't seem to send the message to her face.

The knight was standing over her now. His face was so concerned, so familiar. *Dancing in the living room, and laughing with Mom. Rescue me.*

The knight was her father.

He crouched beside her, lifted her head, stroked her hair.

Oh, God. Is this what forgiveness feels like?

"Gaia?" he whispered. "Gaia, I don't want you to misunderstand. I'm not who you think I am."

She squeezed her eyes shut. *Please don't say that.*

"I'm not Tom. But I'm your family. I'm . . . your father's brother. His twin."

She finally made her mouth work. "His . . . brother?"

The knight nodded. "I've wanted to find you, and take care of you. But I wasn't sure how you'd react. So I waited. Tonight I had no choice but to show myself. I'm sorry if this is painful, Gaia. I'm so sorry. But I'm here now. I'm with you. You're my brother's child. And I love you."

Gaia drank in his words. An elixir. A potion.

She had a family. She could feel the strength returning to her body, with the hope. With the love.

"There's a lot to explain," he whispered, "but I can't now. I have to go. As long as you're safe . . ."

Gaia opened her eyes and looked at him. "No . . ."

He nodded, stroking her hair. "It's all right. You'll understand soon. I promise, I won't be far. I'll come back for you. I swear it."

Gaia struggled to sit up. It was as though her nerves had turned into live electrical wires.

Then her uncle placed one gentle kiss on her forehead, and he was gone.

Don't cry, she told herself, greedily pulling air into her lungs in quick, sharp breaths. Don't.

Her uncle had saved her. Her family.

"Gaia!"

She turned. "Ed?" But before she could ream him for following her, she spotted a figure flinging itself toward Sam.

Her eyes widened. "Don't . . . even . . . tell me."

"She saw the whole thing," Ed said.

Gaia watched Heather pick up the nylon case from where it lay on the ground beside Sam. She watched her place her perfectly manicured hand on his forehead, her perfectly glossed lips on his cheek.

And she watched Sam open his eyes.

She was a good twenty feet away, but even from that distance, Gaia heard his whisper. It seemed to explode in the deepness of the night. "Heather?"

"Yes," sobbed Heather. "I'm here, Sam. I'm here."

Gaia saw him try to smile and she saw his grateful

eyes move from Heather's face to the nylon bag and then back to her face. His voice was trembling with exhaustion and emotion when he asked, "Did you . . . save me?"

Gaia closed her eyes. This wasn't happening.

To her credit, Heather didn't say yes. But she didn't say no, either.

Sam is okay.

He thinks Heather saved him, but he's okay.

CJ's dead.

I didn't kill him, but I saw them zipping up the body bag and hoisting him into the ambulance, so he's dead.

I have an uncle.

I'd never heard of him before today and he's been absent for my entire life—even longer than my dad—but I have an uncle.

Before today I hadn't thought it was possible for life to get any more surreal.

Today proved me very, very wrong.

here is a
sneak peek of
Fearless™ #4:
TWISTED

Sometimes I wonder what
I would say if I were ever asked
out on a date.

You'd think that since it's
never happened to me, I might
have had some time in the past
seventeen years to formulate the
perfect response. You'd think
that with all the movies I'd
seen, I would have at least
picked up some cheesy line. Some
doe-eyed, swooning acceptance.

But I pretty much stay away
from romantic comedies. There's
no relationship advice to be had
from an Arnold Swarzenegger film.

Besides, you can't formulate
the perfect response for a situation you can't remotely imagine.

I figure that if it ever does
happen (not probable) I'll end up
saying something along the lines of,
"Uh," or slight variations thereof.

"Uh . . . unh," if the guy's a freak.

"Uh . . . huh," if the guy's a nonfreak.

I wonder what Heather said to
Sam when he first asked her out.

Probably something disgustingly perfect. Something right out of a movie. Something like, "I was wondering when you'd ask." Or maybe Heather asked Sam out. And he said something like, "It would be my honor."

Okay. Stomach now reacting badly. Must think about something else.

What did Heather say when Ed asked her out?

Okay. Stomach now severely cramping.

So what happens after the "Uh . . . huh"? Awkward pauses, I assume. Idiot small talk, sweaty palms (his), dry mouth (also his), bad food. (I imagine dates don't happen at places where they have good food—like Gray's Papaya or Dojo's.)

And I won't even get into what happens after the most-likely difficult digestion. What does the nonfreak expect at that point? Hand holding? Kissing? Groping? Heavy groping? Sex?

Stomach no longer wishes to be a component of my body.

Must stop here.

Luckily, I won't ever have to deal with any of this. Because no nonfreak will ever ask me out. And no freak will ever get more than the initial grunt.

He was going
to tell **risking**
Gaia Moore
that he **it**
loved her.

EVEN BACK WHEN HIS LEGS WORKED,

Ed had never been fearless.

People who had seen him on
a skateboard or a pair of in-lines
might have been surprised to
hear it. There had been no stairs
too steep to slalom, no handrail
he wasn't willing to challenge, no

The Decision

traffic too thick to dare. Anyone would tell you, Ed
Fargo was a wild man. He took more risks, and
took them faster, than any other boarder in the city.

The dark secret was that all through those days, almost
every second, Ed had been terrified. Every time his wheels
had sent sparks lancing from a metal rail, every time he
had gone over a jump and felt gravity tugging down at his
stomach, Ed had been sure he was about to die.

And when it didn't happen, when he landed, and
lived, and rolled on to skate another day, it had been a
thousand times sweeter just because he had
been so scared. It seemed to Ed that there was nothing
better than that moment after the terror had passed.

Then he lost the use of his legs and grew a wheelchair
on his butt, and everything changed. A wheelchair did
not give the sort of thrills you got from a skateboard.
There had been a few times, especially right after he realized he was never, ever going to get out of
the chair, that Ed had thought about taking the con-
traption out into traffic—just to see how well it played

with the taxis and delivery vans. That kind of thinking was scary in a whole different, definitely less fun way.

Legs or no legs, Ed wasn't sure that any stunt he had pulled in the past had terrified him as much as the one he was about to attempt.

He was going to tell Gaia Moore that he loved her.

Ed had been infatuated with Gaia since he first saw her in the school hallway. He was half smitten as soon as they spoke, and all the way gone within a couple of days.

Since then, Ed and Gaia had become friends—or at least they had come as close to being friends as Gaia's don't-get-close-to-me force fields would allow. To tell Gaia how he really felt would mean risking the relationship they already shared. Ed was horrified by the thought of losing contact with Gaia, but he was determined to take that chance.

For once, he was going to see what it was like to be fearless.

Sour Seventeen

ONE IDIOT AN HOUR. GAIA FIGURED that if they would let her beat up a butt-head per class, it would make the whole day go oh-so-smoothly. She would get nervous energy out of her system, add a few high points to her dull-as-a-bowling-ball day, and by the time the final bell rang the world would have eight fewer losers. All good things.

It might also help her keep her mind off Sam Moon. Sam whose life she had saved more than once. Sam who was oblivious to her existence. Sam who had the biggest bitch this side of Fifth Avenue for a girlfriend, but didn't seem to notice.

And still, Gaia couldn't stop thinking about him. Apparently, somewhere along the line, she had also been taught self-torture.

Gaia trudged out of her third-period class and shouldered her way though the clogged hallway with her cruise control completely engaged. Every conscious brain cell was dedicated to the ongoing task of what to do about her irritating and somewhat embarrassing Sam Problem.

It was like a drug problem, only slightly less messy.

Gaia tried to sidetrack her consciousness with a number of past favorites:

- How much she hated school
- How much she hated Ella
- How much she hated her father

And the newest:

- How much she hated Heather Gannis

And the fact that Heather had had sex with Sam. And the fact that Heather had taken the credit for saving Sam. And the fact that Heather got to hold hands with Sam and kiss Sam and talk to Sam and—

Gaia came to a stop in front of her locker and kicked it hard, denting the bottom of the door. A couple of Gap girls turned to stare, so Gaia kicked it again. The Gap girls scurried away.

She glared at her vague reflection in the battered door. In the dull metal, she was only an outline. That's all she was to Sam. A vague shadow of nothing much. A joke.

For a few delusional days, Gaia had thought Sam might be the one. The one to break her embarrassing record as the only unkissed seventeen-year-old on planet Earth. Maybe even the one to turn sex from something as hypothetical as the equations in calculus class into a good, solid, warm reality. But it wasn't going to happen.

There was not going to be any sex. There was never going to be any kissing. Not with Sam. Not ever.

Gaia popped the door of her locker open, tossed in the books she was carrying and took out another at random without bothering to look at it. Then she slammed the door just as hard as she had kicked it.

The poor locker door looked like someone had used it as a trampoline.

This was it.

Gaia had to get her shit together before more help-less inanimate objects suffered the same fate.

She squeezed her eyes shut for a moment, squeezed hard, as if she could squeeze out her unwanted thoughts.

Even though Gaia knew zilch about love, knew less about relationships, and knew even less about psychology, she knew exactly what her girlfriends, if she had any, would tell her.

Find a new guy. Someone to distract you. Someone who cares about you.

Right. No problem.

Unfortunately it had taken her seventeen years to find a guy who didn't care about her.

NAVIGATION OF HIGH SCHOOL HALL-

ways takes on a whole new meaning when you're three feet wide and mounted on wheels.

Ed Fargo skidded around a corner, narrowly avoided a collision with a janitor, then spun right past a knot of students laughing at

The Attempt

some private joke. He threw the chair into hard reverse and did a quick 180 to dodge a stream of band students lugging instruments out a doorway, then he powered through a gap, coasted down a ramp, and took the next corner so hard he went around on one wheel.

Fifty feet away, Gaia Moore was just shutting the door of her locker. Ed let the chair coast to a halt as he watched her. Gaia's football shirt was wrinkled and her socks didn't match. Most of her pale hair had slipped free of whatever she had been using to hold it into a ponytail. Loose strands hovered around the sculpted planes of her face and the remaining hair gathered at the back of her head in a heavy, tangled, tumbled mass.

She was the most beautiful thing that Ed had ever seen.

He gave the wheels of his chair a sharp push and darted ahead of some slow walkers. Before Gaia could take two steps, Ed was at her side.

"Looking for your next victim?" he asked.

Gaia glanced down, and for a moment the characteristic frown on her insanely perfect lips was replaced by a smile. "Hey, Ed. What's up?"

Ed almost turned around and left. Why should he push it? He could live on that smile for at least a month.

Fearless, he told himself. Be fearless.

"I guess you don't want us to win at basketball this year," he started, trying to keep the tone light.

Gaia looked puzzled. "What?"

"The guy you went after this morning, Brad Reston," Ed continued. "He's a starting forward."

"How did you hear about it?" The frown was back full force.

"From Darla Rigazzim," Ed answered. "She's talked you up in every class this morning."

"Yeah, well. I wish she wouldn't." She looked away and started up the hallway again, the smooth muscles of her legs stretching under faded jeans.

Ed kept pace for fifty feet. Twice he opened his mouth to say something, but he shut it again before a word escaped. There was a distant, distracted look on Gaia's face now. The moment had passed. He would have to wait.

No, a voice said from the back of his mind. Don't wait. Tell her now. Tell her everything.

"Gaia . . . ," he started.

Something in his tone must have caught Gaia's attention. She stopped in the middle of one long stride and turned to him. Her right eyebrow was raised and her changing eyes were as blue-gray as the Atlantic fifty miles off the coast. "What's wrong, Ed?"

Ed swallowed. Suddenly he felt as if he were back on his skateboard, ready to challenge the bumpy ride down another flight of steps—only the steps in front of him went down, and down, and down forever.

Ed shook his head. "It's not important."

I love you.

"Nothing at all, really."

I want to be with you.

"Just . . . nothing in particular."

I want you to be with me.

"I'll talk to you after class."

Gaia stared at him for a moment longer, then nodded. "All right. I'll see you later." She turned around and walked off quickly, her long legs eating up the distance.

"Perfect," Ed whispered to her retreating back. A perfect pair, he thought. She's brave to the point of almost being dangerous, and I'm gutless to the point of almost being depressing.

And with
those words,
Gaia's

painfully

seventeen-

beautiful

year streak

officially

came to an

end.

THE SCHEDULE WAS A XEROX.

The Offer

Maybe a Xerox of a Xerox. Whatever it was, the print was so faint and muddy that David Twain had to squint hard and hold the sheet of paper up to the light just to make out a few words.

He lowered the folded page and looked around him. People were streaming past on all sides. The students at this school were visibly different. They moved faster. Talked faster. Dressed like they expected a society photographer to show up at any minute. They were, David thought, probably all brain-dead.

Still, nobody else seemed to be having a hard time finding the right room. Of course, the rest of them had probably spent more than eight minutes in the building.

A bell rang right over his head. The sound was so loud that it seemed to jar the fillings in his teeth. David winced and glanced up at the clanging bell. That was when he noticed that the number above the door and the room number on the schedule were the same.

A half dozen students slipped past David as he stood, stunned, in the doorway. He turned to follow, caught a bare glimpse of movement from the corner of his eye, and the next thing he knew he was flying through the air.

11

He landed hard on his butt. All at once he bit his tongue, dropped his books, and let out a sound that reminded him of a small dog that's been kicked. The books skidded twenty feet, letting out a spray of loose papers as they went.

The bell stopped ringing. In the space of seconds, the remaining students in the hallway dived into classrooms. David found himself alone.

`Almost.`

"Sorry."

It was a mumbled apology. Not much conviction there.

David looked up to see a tall girl with loose, thick blond hair staring down at him. "Yeah," he said. There was a warm, salty taste in his mouth. Blood. And his butt ached from the fall. At the moment those things `didn't matter.`

"You okay?" the girl asked, shoving her hand in her pocket and looking as if she'd rather be anywhere but here.

"Yeah," he said again, reaching back to touch his spine. "I'm fine. Great."

The girl shook her head. "If you say so." Her tousled hair spilled down across her shoulders as she reached down to him.

"Thanks." David let her help him to his feet. The girl's palm was warm. Her fingers surprisingly strong. "What did I run into?"

"Me."

David blinked. "You knocked me down?"

The blond girl shrugged and released his hand. "I didn't do it on purpose."

"You must have been moving pretty fast to hit that hard." David resisted an urge to rub his aches. Instead, he offered the hand the girl had just released. "Hi, I'm David Twain."

The girl glanced over her shoulder at the classroom, then stared at David's fingers as if she'd never experienced a handshake before.

"Gaia," she said. "Gaia Moore." She took his hand in hers and gave it a single quick shake.

David was the one who had fallen, but for some reason the simple introduction was enough to make this girl, this painfully beautiful girl, seem awkward.

"Great name," he said. "Like the earth goddess."

"Yeah, well." The girl looked down at the floor and shrugged before glancing back at David. "If you're okay, I need to get to class."

David shook his head. "No," he said.

Gaia blinked. "What?"

"No," David repeated. "I'm not okay." He leaned toward her and lowered his voice to his best thick whisper. "I won't be okay until you agree to go to dinner with me tomorrow night."

"UH . . . HUH."

The Response

"What?" David asked, his very clear blue eyes narrowing.

He was a male. He was, apparently, a nonfreak. He was not Sam. He got the affirmative grunt before Gaia could even remind herself of the ramifications.

"I said, uh-huh," Gaia said evenly, lifting her chin.

"Good," he said. "There's this place called Cookies & Couscous. It's more like a bakery than a restaurant. You know it?"

Of course she knew it. Any place that had cookies in its name and was located within twenty miles of George and Ella's automatically went on Gaia's mental map. "On Thompson."

"Right." He nodded and a piece of black hair fell over his forehead. "We can eat baklava, wash it down with espresso, and worry about having a main course after we're full of dessert."

"When?" she said. Oh, good, Gaia. Look eager. Look eager when you're anything but.

He smiled. "Tomorrow? Eight o'clock."

Gaia nodded almost imperceptibly.

His smile widened. "It's a date."

And with those words, Gaia's seventeen-year streak officially came to an end.

14

I AM AN IDIOT.

Gaia stared down at the toes of her battered sneakers and wondered how long it would be before she threw up. Or ran out of the room. Or exploded.

Maybe Connecticut

Taking a date from a guy you had known all of ten seconds seemed like such a desperate thing. A total loser move. Like something a girl who was seventeen and had never been kissed might do. The whole thing was starting to make her more than a little nauseated.

Who knew what this David guy expected out of her? Gaia the undated. Gaia the unkissed. Gaia the ultimate virgin.

Maybe it was a setup. Maybe Heather and some of the certified Popular Crowd (also known as The Association of People Who Really Hate Gaia Moore) had put this guy in her way just so they could pop up at her so-called date and pull a *Carrie*.

Gaia closed her eyes. Stupid. Definitely stupid.

"Uh, you're Gaia Moore, right?"

Gaia looked up from her desk and found a tall blond girl standing in front of her. From the way people were up and moving around the room, class had to be over. Gaia had successfully managed to nondaydream away the entire period.

15

"Are you Gaia?"

"Uh, yeah." Gaia was surprised on two counts. First was that the girl knew her name at all, the second was that she actually pronounced it right on the first try. "Yeah, that's right."

"I'm Cassie," said the girl. "Cassie Greenman."

How wonderful for you, thought Gaia. She had noticed the girl in class before. Though she hadn't seen her running with the core Popular People crowd, Gaia assumed that Cassie was in on the Anti-Gaia Coalition.

"Aren't you worried?" asked Cassie.

"What am I supposed to be worried about?" asked Gaia. She wondered if she had missed the announcement of a history exam or some similar nonevent. Or maybe this girl was talking about Gaia's upcoming date. Maybe Heather and her pals really were planning some horrible heap of humiliation. Maybe they were all standing outside the door right now, ready to mock Gaia for thinking someone would actually ask her out. Not that Gaia cared.

The girl rolled her eyes. "About being next."

"The next what?" Gaia asked.

"You know." Cassie raised a hand to her throat and drew one silver-blue-painted fingernail across the pale skin of her throat. "Being the next one killed."

Killed. That was a word that definitely drew Gaia's attention. She sat up straighter in her desk. "What do you mean, killed?"

"Killed. Like in dead."

"Killed by who?"

The blond girl rolled her eyes. "By the Gentleman."

Gaia began to wonder if everyone had just gone nuts while she wasn't paying attention. "Why would a gentleman want to kill me?"

"Not *a* gentleman," Cassie said. "*The* Gentleman. You know—the serial killer." She didn't add, "Duh," but it was clear enough in her voice.

Now Gaia was definitely interested. "Tell me about it."

"Haven't you heard? Everyone's been talking about it all morning."

"They haven't been talking to me."

Cassie shrugged. "There's this guy killing girls. He killed two over in New Jersey and three more somewhere in . . . I don't know, maybe Connecticut."

"So?" said Gaia. "Why should I be worried about what happens in Connecticut?"

That drew another roll of the eyes from the blond girl. "Don't you ever listen to the news? Last night he killed a girl from the university right over on the MacDougal side of the park."

Now Gaia wasn't just interested, she was offended. The park in question was Washington Square Park, and that was Gaia's territory. Her home court. Since coming to New York, she had been living in an old brownstone with George and Ella Niven. But the room at the top of the brownstone was not home. Washington Square Park was home.

From the chessboards to the playground, all of it was hers. She used it as a place to relax, and as a place to hunt city vermin. Gaia had been in the park herself the night before, just hoping for muggers and dealers to give her trouble. She had found nothing. The idea that someone had been killed just a block away made the muscles at the back of her jaw draw tight.

"How do they know it was the same guy?" she asked.

"Because of what he . . . does to them," her informant replied with an overdone shiver. "I don't know about you, but I'm dyeing my hair jet black till this guy is caught."

"Why?"

Cassie was starting to look a little exasperated. She pulled out a lock of her wavy hair and held it in front of her face. "Hello? Because all the victims had the same color hair, that's why. You need to be careful, too."

"I'm not that blond," said Gaia.

"Are you nuts? Your hair's even lighter than mine." The girl gave her a little smile. "It's not too different, though. In fact, ever since you started here, people have been telling me how much we look alike. Like you could be my sister or something."

Gaia stared at the girl. Whoever had said she looked like Gaia needed to get their eyes checked. Cassie Greenman was patently pretty. Very pretty. There was no way Gaia looked anything like her.

"You're nothing like me."

Cassie frowned. "You don't think . . ."

"No."

"I think we would look a lot alike," insisted Cassie. "If you would . . . you know . . . like, clean up . . . and dress better and—" She shrugged. "You know."

All Gaia knew was that all the cleaning up and good clothes in the world wouldn't stop her from looking like an overmuscled freak. She wished she was beautiful like her mother had been, but she would settle for being pretty like Cassie. She would settle for being normal. "Thanks for giving me the heads up on this killer."

Cassie wrinkled her nose. "Isn't it creepy? Do you think he's still around here?"

"I wouldn't worry too much." Gaia stood up and grabbed for her books. "If he's still here, he won't be for long."

Not in my park, she thought. If the killer was still there, Gaia intended to find him and stop him.

Suddenly she felt pinpricks of excitement moving over her skin. For the first time all day, she felt fully awake. Fully engaged. Fully there. She needed to make a plan. She needed to make sure that if this guy attacked anyone else in the park, it was Gaia.

As terrible as it was, in a weird sort of way the news about the serial killer actually made Gaia feel better. At least she had stopped thinking about her date.